A PILGRIMAGE TO DEATH

A REVEREND CICI GURULE MYSTERY

BOOK 1

ALEXA PADGETT

Edited by Heather Myers and Nicole Pomeroy
Cover Design by Emma Rider at Moonstruck Cover Design
& Photography

ISBN: 978-1-945090-22-6

For Rebecca. Thank you for believing I had this story in me.

To Jackie,
Happy Reading!
Alexa Padgett

1

Suspicion always haunts the guilty mind.
— *Shakespeare*

Cecilia Gurule was a reverend for God's sake. She dealt in souls—the broken, empty, seeking, and, yes, the dead.

Bodies? Not her wheelhouse.

At least they weren't until that Tuesday afternoon when *Domine Deus* decided to test both her faith and her life.

She came within a bullet of losing both.

Cecilia, who much preferred Cici, met Sam in the parking lot of the Aspen Vista Trail. She was late. Not really her fault, but typical, thanks to her parishioners' unwillingness to accept Tuesdays as her one day per week away from the church.

Wide and rocky, the trail snaked over eleven miles up the side of the mountain following an old forest service road. While the incline was never scramble steep, it rose at a consistent pace, switching back with views toward the city or up to the ski basin. A few narrow runnels of water—not big enough to be considered creeks—dribbled from the remaining snowpack.

Cici suggested it last week because both she and Sam had the weekday off, meaning fewer hikers on the bottom part of the trail, and they could spend the three-plus hours needed to reach the summit.

Unfortunately, Cici suggested the trail before she made plans to breakfast with the widowed Mrs. Sanchez, whose son worked out at the state penitentiary on NM-14.

"I don't understand these kids." Mrs. Sanchez wiped her mouth with her napkin, leaving a smear of bright red on the paper. Her lips were the same light bronze as her craggy skin, hints of the crimson lipstick settled into the faint lines bisecting her lower lip.

"Juanito has one more year at that fancy private school. He has a pretty girlfriend. Yet he cannot be happy? He causes his father such heartache, Reverend." She picked up her coffee mug and shoved it toward Cici. "You talk to the boy for his father. Set him straight."

"I'll do what I can, Mrs. Sanchez."

"Humph." The woman set her mug down with a crack, her dark, deep-set eyes glaring from between folds of skin. Without the bright lipstick, her mouth seemed hidden under the wrinkles.

"I'm old, Reverend. I cannot control the boy. His father, Miguel, spent most of the last year picking up extra shifts for the tuition at St. Michaels. Juanito needs to respect the rules we set for him."

"Which are?" Cici asked.

Mrs. Sanchez tossed her napkin onto her plate with the half-finished breakfast burrito. Cici picked up her own warm tortilla and bit into the wrap, enjoying the spicy flavors of green chile and sausage. One thing about Mrs. Sanchez: she was a fine cook.

"No seeing that girl past ten p.m. Good grades—all A's so that he's ready to go to Tech in a year. That's what he needs—a good education, more choices. Not this…this mess with girls."

"He did receive all A's last year, and it's summer break now. Shouldn't Juan have the chance to focus on his job or maybe even spend time with Jaycee?"

"No more time with the girlfriend," Mrs. Sanchez said with a sharp motion of her hand. "That's how I'll end up a great-grand-mother. The boy needs more school. He is not yet eighteen." Her face crumpled. "He is the age we lost his brother, Marco, Reverend. You know this. Juan is all the family has left."

———

"Who was it this time?" Sam Chastain, Cici's friend and hiking partner, asked. He pulled on a tattered ball cap—probably the one Cici's twin sister, Anna Carmen, gave him years ago—and pulled on his backpack, settling it comfortably over his gray Red River T-shirt.

His short, dark ponytail stuck through the hole in the back like a bristle-brush. He slid on a pair of Ray-Bans to protect his gunmetal-blue eyes.

"Mrs. Sanchez. I got a great breakfast out of the deal."

"She want you to have the talk with Juan?" Sam asked.

Sam was a detective with the Santa Fe Police department and fellow search-and-rescue teammate. The two had known each other for decades. Cici grabbed her water bottle and checked her sneakers.

"Got a hat?" Sam asked. "You know you're going to burn if you don't wear one."

Sam studied her features, his gaze resting on her high cheek-bones that always burned thanks to the pale skin Cici and her sister inherited from their mother, along with the oval shape of her face and the long-lashed hazel eyes.

"Yep," Cici said, settling the cap on her head and pulling her long, jet-black pony tail through the hole in the back.

Sam offered her a radio, which she took, clipping it to her thick, brown leather belt.

"Why are we carrying these?"

Sam shrugged. "Boss man wants everyone on the trails wearing 'em. Maybe because of the helicopter extraction earlier this year?"

They started up the trail, moving in tandem as if they'd been hiking together for years.

"She's recovered," Cici said. "I called the woman who fell off Big Tesuque and talked to her. Her ankle's out of the cast."

"Lot of ruckus for a broken ankle and some bruises," Sam replied.

"She slid four hundred feet into that ravine, Sam. Cut the woman some slack."

"Stupid to hike alone, and you know it. We wouldn't have had to waste so many resources on her if she'd been smarter."

Cici did, but her job was to see others' points of view, to help them grow, both in their humanity and spirituality. Refusing to get pulled further into an argument with Sam, she continued to hike.

They matched pace for a while in companionable silence. Cici began to feel…not sad. She hadn't been happy since Anna Carmen's death. But in this moment, with the sun shining and the aspens whispering overhead, Cici's lips lifted at the corners.

The call came over the radio clipped to her belt. The same message squawked from Sam's radio. He stopped, his chest expanding with each hard breath. They'd hiked the steepest part of the Aspen Trail. Sam wiped the sweat off his brow and pulled in a deep breath. He unlatched his walkie-talkie and pressed the button on the side.

"Repeat that, please."

"Missing hiker. Wife called it in when she got off the mountain."

"She left him out here by himself?" Cici asked, already wrinkling her nose in disgust. People continued to disappoint her.

Sam shook his head. "Not now, Cici. What's the trail?"

"Aspen Vista," the voice said over the bits of static.

"We're on it. Name, age, any other stats?"

"I know." The voice crackled but the exasperation was clear even through the bad connection. "Donald…fifty…complain… heart."

"Uh oh," Cici murmured.

"Last known whereabouts?" Sam asked.

"The summit."

"Why'd the wife leave him there?" Cici muttered. "If he was in distress when she left him, he might not have survived while she strolled down the mountain."

"Later," Sam replied. He pressed the "Talk" button. "We're a quarter mile from that location. Cici and I will start the sweep."

"Roger…full crew coming in."

"Great. From what you said, we'll probably need it. Over

and out." Sam clipped the thick black radio to his belt again. He turned back to look at Cici, who'd crossed her arms and scowled down into the valley below.

"None of that, Cee. Not all people are your parents."

"No, shit, detective," she grunted.

"Hey," Sam said, bumping her shoulder with his in a gentle gesture she'd come to expect from him over the last few years.

While they'd spent time together before her twin's death, Cici made a point to seek him out more often after Anna Carmen's funeral—especially once she'd made the decision to quit as the associate reverend from the large, wealthy church outside Boston—and move back home. He'd reciprocated by always being available, even during the difficult transition when he left the promising position on a joint task force in Denver. He'd been so excited to participate in that work because only the best people from the region were chosen, and Sam was one of the youngest. But, after explaining the situation to his boss, Agent Klein helped Sam move back in the detective bureau in Santa Fe.

"Priests aren't supposed to use that kind of language," he said.

Cici bumped him back, harder. Five male cousins within three years of her own age taught her a few important details—like how to fight dirty. "I'm not a priest. And not just because of my reproductive organs. I'm a reverend."

"With a predilection for curse words and a willingness to abuse your fellow man," Sam said over his shoulder as he moved back into point position on the trail. He made a tsking sound. "C'mon, Rev. Let's go rescue our guy. Maybe you'll make the front page of the paper. Again." He turned to wink, his lips lifting when Cici rolled his eyes.

"Ugh. One time, Sam."

"That's all it took for me to be able to tease you about it for the rest of your life." He started to chuckle. "Whatever happened to the chicken?"

Cici glared while Sam struggled to keep a straight face.

"I don't know." She huffed. "Hopefully, it's living a long, chicken-y life."

She rolled her eyes again and began to climb; Sam fell into step to the left and a half-foot in front of her.

Sam's foot shifted as loose slag slid out from under his thick-soled hiking boot. He slowed his pace, taking more care with where he stepped. No point in getting hurt on the way up—that would just make more work for the SAR crew already on its way.

"I can't believe that little girl asked you to bless a chicken at the Pet Parade."

"This is Santa Fe. Home of animal lovers and weirdness."

And murder.

Even though the sun beat down in thick, hot rays, Cici shivered. Something about this entire situation felt…well, off. She picked up the thread of their conversation to give herself something to do besides watch where she placed her feet and worry about what they'd find.

"Anyway, Yale wasn't big on the cussing. Manhattan and Boston are where I picked up some choice words."

"You were supposed to show those sinners how to rise above coarse language, sin, and all that shit."

Cici shrugged. Not new ground here. She and Sam had bickered for years. That wasn't saying much, really. She'd known most of the people in Santa Fe for years.

The aspen leaves rippled in the wind—a soft, fluttering roll of vegetation that sounded like a gentle, low tide—a strange phenomenon common here, high up in the Santa Fe National Forest where blue sky and slender white tree trunks seemed to merge. Typically, the sound soothed her.

Not now that she'd thought about her sister. The ache left by Anna Carmen's death seemed to grow and weep, just as it always did when thoughts of her twin blindsided her.

Cici lifted her leg high to take her up to the next rock as sweat trickled down the middle of her back and her thighs began to ache with the deliciousness of hard use.

Cici cleared her head and organized her thoughts on these weekly hikes. Spending time outdoors with Sam became a weekly ritual more than six months ago. She looked forward to these hours-long jaunts because they helped her prepare a better sermon.

They turned the last sharp curve and Sam's feet planted firmly into the path, blocking her view. He cursed—worse than her words. Cici's heart hammered and the dread in her stomach shifted, heaving, as Cici edged around him.

"Wait, Cee. You don't want to see this."

Too late—and not as if she would have listened. Her throat tightened as she stared into the sightless eyes of Donald Johnson, one of the founding members of the church she'd taken over earlier this year.

A gust of wind slammed against her overheated skin and the soft rustling of the aspens built into the crash of waves. Or maybe it was her ears, thrumming with the rush of blood to her head.

She barely heard Sam call in their location.

Rigor mortis had already come and left his body before she and Sam found him, toppled off the large boulder, his stainless-steel canteen overturned and empty at his feet. The water stained the ground and his right hiking boot, making the leather darker, near black. Near as black as the blood on the rock and stuck to his Lobos T-shirt, trailing down onto his designer jeans.

Sam's hand came down on her shoulder and she flinched, hard, but she didn't look away from Donald. Two narrow gashes showed pink and a trickle of blood. His hands—large and hairy—nicked from the blade. A longer, deeper gash split open the meaty part of his hand almost as if he'd grappled with the blade.

But Cici focused on the large wolf logo. The UNM mascot seemed to have opened its mouth right above a wound in his back, ready to devour him.

Or maybe Cici, with memories of another murder. That wound...

2

Misery acquaints a man with strange bedfellows.
— Shakespeare

Not again. But before she could stop it, Cici slid back to the evening of the call. She hadn't been in the state, but she'd already been at the airport, trying to buy her way on to a flight—any flight—because that place inside Cici where Anna Carmen lived had gone silent.

Cici and Anna Carmen had figured out the connection as toddlers, maybe earlier. They didn't need to be in the same room to check in with each other, and as they matured, they didn't need to be in the same building or even the same state. Their connection wasn't exactly an unspoken communication—more that the girls were so in tune with each other's thoughts and emotions.

But that afternoon, Anna Carmen had seemed to fade from Cici's consciousness. Not a gentle easing—more of a great gasp of despair and regret.

And then, nothing.

Cici had been with her boyfriend the moment of Anna Carmen's stabbing, working on the location in Central America they wanted to explore for Cici and Lyndon's first field work trip together. A recent Harvard graduate, who'd finished his post-doctoral work in archaeology, Lyndon had asked Cici if she'd go with him if he got the funding. She hadn't been too sure if she should.

He'd proven to be unrelenting in his arguments, just as he was in most other areas of his life. When Lyndon discussed the forest's health and how it impacted the natives' way of life, Cici's desire to remove herself from his all-consuming focus turned to interest.

Lyndon knew Cici wanted to study the forests in Peru, assess their health and the balance with the natives living in the high region of the area. Cici's master's degree shared a dual focus in divinity and environmental studies. She'd interned as an associate reverend outside Boston, and the church hired her as an associate pastor as soon as she'd graduated. For the last year and a half of her internship, she hadn't been able to focus on her environmental science degree, but she had met Lyndon at a group on spirituality and environmentalism she moderated the year before, and he'd opened the door for her to focus on both of her passions.

After many conversations with her sister, she'd accepted the opportunity. Lyndon had been ecstatic, coming up with potential scenarios for their work—and living arrangements. Many of which pushed Cici even further outside her comfort zone.

But, by then, she'd agreed, and the situation had already snowballed.

At the time, Cici had been much more excited about an adventure in Peru, even if she had to put up with Lyndon's intensity, than taking over the church back in her hometown. Though, both her sister and many of her lifelong friends lobbied hard for her to return home.

But Cici hadn't wanted to return to the place where her mother lost not just her marriage and dignity, but also her battle with cancer.

Then, when the connection to her sister had popped, Cici collapsed, passed out still hearing her name cried in a soft, broken voice, her twin's name leaking past her stiff lips. She'd woken on the small couch in her apartment, shivering, aching, as if she had the flu.

But it was worse than an illness. A portion of Cici ripped from her soul and she'd never recovered. Never *could* recover.

*Anna Carmen, Aci…*Cici slid back into the pet name she'd created for her sister when they were quite young and Cici couldn't say "Carmen." *Don't leave me.*

How many times had she said that aloud and deep within her soul? Too many. And her sister never heard or never listened because the place Anna Carmen had always nourished remained black, blank, silent no matter how many times Cici struggled to reconnect.

In desperation and against Lyndon's loud objections, Cici had stood, then struggled to right herself, right the world. She left the apartment as fast as she could.

As her sister's closest relative, the only one alive to care that she was gone, Cici had received *the call* before Anna Carmen's boyfriend had. She'd cried from the moment she'd heard the words, where a ticket agent, also tearing up, managed to find her a seat on the next available flight. She'd wept through the entire flight to Albuquerque, not that it changed the new reality she'd have to live with.

That she *still* lived with.

Thank goodness by the time she'd landed, Evan—Anna Carmen's boyfriend—and a few other close friends had taken care of the preliminary issues. Sam had met her at the airport and pulled her into a long, tight hug that signaled a shift in their relationship.

Cici leaned on that shift so heavily right now.

"I'm sorry, Cici." Sam's voice bit through her haze, reconnecting her with the here, the now. Up on top of Aspen Vista Trail, on a sunny late May morning.

"I know this has to bring it all back up," he said, his voice mournful.

Oh, it did. For Sam, too. Sam and her sister had been the best of friends long before Sam and Cici were. In fact, Sam and Cici were friends now by default. That's what losing the most important person in your life did—it created unbreakable bonds between people who'd never been particularly close before.

Well…not for Cici and her sister's boyfriend, Evan. But that was a different story, a different relationship.

A different set of regrets and what-ifs.

Sam turned her toward his chest, but Cici's eyes remained on Donald's body.

"He was stabbed," Cici said.

"Multiple times," Sam said, his eyes that of a clinician—so cold and detached from what had been a living, breathing person.

Cici panted. "That one. In the back."

Sam's hand squeezed her fingers tighter, steadying her. "Yeah."

"It's like…The placement. It's like Anna Carmen."

"Yeah."

Normally, Cici didn't mind Sam's minimal use of language, but now—right now—she needed more.

"Through the kidney," she said, her voice sharpening.

"Looks like," Sam replied as he began to rock her back and forth, back and forth. The soft sway calmed her somewhat.

Much as she wanted to pound Sam with her fists, she couldn't look away from Donald's glazed eyes. An ant crawled over the pale skin of Donald's nose. She shuddered, still unable to look away even as the ant settled on Donald's sclera. Cici shuddered, breaking the strange spell.

She stared up into Sam's face. "What does that *mean*?"

Sam dropped his hands from her back and sighed. He motioned Cici away from the rock where Donald sprawled. When she didn't move, he nudged her, much like a sheep dog, to herd her away from the body, onto the trail, keeping them away from much of the area surrounding the boulder and Donald.

Cici wrapped her arms tight around her waist as she struggled to keep her breakfast burrito in her stomach.

"Good thing you left your dogs home today. They'd mess up the area."

Cici stiffened. "I couldn't take them to the Sanchez's house—she would have beat me with her broom after she cursed at the dogs for shedding. And you know Rodolfo and Mona are well behaved."

"Never said they weren't. Just that the forensic team is more likely to find something if we don't disturb the area. And the dogs would've been all over this guy, messing with evidence."

"Like the ants."

Sam grimaced, turning to face her.

Cici huddled against the rock outcropping where she and Sam leaned, willing her body to ward off the chill of memory. Not even the intensity of May sun at nearly ten thousand feet managed to do so. She shivered and her teeth began to chatter.

"Sam, what does that stab wound mean?" Cici asked again.

"I'm not sure," he said, his voice hesitant.

"But if you had to guess?"

"They fought. You can see that in his defensive wounds on his hands."

Cici shuddered.

"I can't tell you for sure right now Cici," Sam muttered.

"The wound in his back. It's the same as Anna Carmen's."

Sam took off his ball cap and ran his palm over the back of his head, smoothing the wisps of dark hair back into his stubby pony tail just below his crown. The bottom half of his hair was close-cropped. Conservative. Much like his dress slacks and the ties he now wore to work. Those long-sleeve button downs hid his half-sleeve tattoo that slipped in and out of visibility under his sweat-soaked T-shirt.

He'd become as much of an enigma as she had, hiding too many of his feelings and thoughts deep behind those gunmetal eyes and the unusual hair style.

Sam drew in a deep breath, his face as ashen as hers must be. In this, they understood each other.

"I don't know if that was intentional," Sam said.

Cici waited, sensing he had more to say.

"Some murderers have signatures and perhaps this is one. If so…if it's like Anna Carmen's…we could find out more about the killer."

Bring him to justice.

Sam didn't say it, but both he and Cici thought it.

"How would you know? If it's the same."

Sam bit into the cuticle on the side of his left thumb—a sure sign of his increasing agitation. She hadn't seen him do that in a long time. Not since…not since he'd driven her to Anna Carmen's house the night of her murder.

"Forensic evidence."

Cici was sure there was more but Sam clamped his lips tight.

"You're sure?" she asked. "I mean, that there's a possibility to catch her killer?"

Sam blew out a breath. "I don't want you to get your hopes up, Cee."

Cici clenched her jaw to keep the hysterical laughter from bubbling up and over.

"A man I know is dead just there." She pointed. "I don't think my hopes are going to rise any time soon."

"Fine. Based on my preliminary review of the scene." Sam emphasized the word *preliminary*. "Yes, I'd say it's like Anna Carmen's."

"You're sure?"

He ran his hands down his cheeks and turned so he couldn't meet her gaze. "I sometimes look at her file. To remember why I'm here."

Somehow, those words triggered the latte Cici had indulged in earlier this morning. She turned, palm flat on the smooth, white bark of the aspen as her breakfast flowed upward. She wiped her lips with the bandana she kept in her back pocket.

"Shit, Sam."

After a brief attempt to regulate her breathing, Cici grabbed her water bottle and slugged back some of the cool liquid. Her stomach gurgled rebelliously. She ignored it just as she ignored the pain squeezing at her heart. She stared at Donald, but she saw her sister's small body there on those blood-stained stones.

"I mean…" Cici hauled in some air. "Thank you. For caring. But, dammit, give me a chance to prepare for that kind of devotion."

She tipped her head back and squinted up through the leaves.

Sam's eyes remained dark but his tone turned rueful. "I hear the team coming up the trail. They don't need to hear your potty mouth, Reverend Gurule."

Cici bit her lip as she stepped back, flush against the rock wall. The granite poked into her back even as the stone warmed her. Cici shut her eyes. Still light, tinged golden with the perfect summer sun, filtered through her lids. She squeezed them tighter, trying to block out the images of her dead sister's eyes.

No use.

Anna Carmen's bright hazel eyes, Cici's eyes, melded with Donald's darker ones. Different shape but both seemed to beseech her. Their stories intertwined. Death took them in brutal fashion. Too soon.

Much too soon.

Cici's lids fluttered open, and she peered into the canopy of acid-green leaves rustling in a soft, sweet wave. Splashes of bright blue and wisps of white clouds completed the pattern.

For the first time in one year, two months and nine days, Cici felt Anna Carmen next to her. Just as Anna Carmen had nestled in close at her funeral, buoying Cici in that time of need, but not the full-throttle Anna Carmen Cici remembered.

Until now. When her sister lit up her brain and set every cell in Cici's body on fire.

"Anna Carmen," Cici whispered.

She shifted, turning her head, unsurprised to find her twin standing there next to her.

The silence lengthened as her sister regarded her, eyes urgent. Cici reached out, needing to touch her twin, but Anna Carmen shook her head, moving backward. She dipped her head toward Donald even as she began to fade.

Through the soft rustle of the leaves in the trees, Anna Carmen's voice whispered back, "You need to help Sam. You need to fix what I broke."

"What's wrong, Cee?" Sam asked, crouching next to her, where she'd slid down the rock face.

"Come back," Cici murmured, continuing to stare at the location just next to the thick white trunk where her sister had been.

"Cici?" Sam's voice became more urgent. "Look at me. Are you in shock?"

With great effort, she wrenched her gaze from the now-empty spot and met Sam's concerned eyes.

"No."

"You sure? You look like…well, you like you saw a ghost."

Cici stood, her legs wobbly but able to hold her glanced back at the area where her sister had stood.

"I did," she murmured. "But that's not the worst of it."

Probably for the best one of the SAR volunteers called Sam's name before she spoke again. His attention shifted to the lanky fifty-something retiree from Nevada.

Anna Carmen wanted Cici to find her killer. Donald's killer, too.

Because Anna Carmen's emotions pointed to one clear realization: if Cici failed, more deaths would follow.

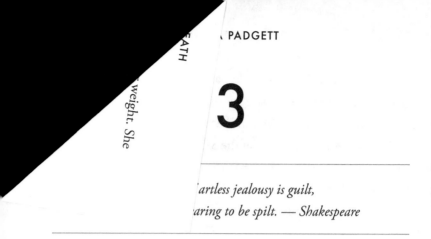

3

artless jealousy is guilt,
aring to be spilt. — Shakespeare

Death stalks.

Not a realization anyone should need to make. Death sucked, too. But, now, eighteen hours after finding Donald, Cici had had to talk about finding him, about her sister, and everything related to leaving this mortal coil to pretty much everyone in the Santa Fe Police Department and Search and Rescue—plus a few others who came up the trail just for kicks.

Cici never wanted to discuss wounds or death or dying again. Kind of a problem for a reverend.

She laid her head on her paper-strewn wooden desk and closed her gritty eyes. They popped back open immediately as her stomach heaved.

Thankfully, it settled again before she had to bolt from her small second room at the back of her house into the equally small bathroom off the narrow hall.

Eyes. Donald's and Anna Carmen's.

Not even Rodolfo's and Mona's warm bodies and doggie breaths alleviated the terror and grief of reliving those moments after Cici learned her twin sister was dead.

Sam had offered to stay with her, but Cici's casita was definitely *ita*. As in tiny—and having Sam stay the night to comfort her felt weird. Because she wanted him to. Desperately. So, Cici sent him home.

Which meant Cici slept little last night. And today, she paid for that decision with a pounding head and raw eyelids.

She glanced at the clock, relieved she needed to head over to the church. Hopefully, Sam would call her as soon as he had more information about Donald's death…and what it meant for her sister's murder investigation.

———

"You got a minute?" Carole, the church secretary, asked.

Cici smiled as Carole's gray head poked into her doorway. The older woman wore green cat-eye glasses. The beaded chain that wrapped around the delicate silver eye pieces jangled.

Cici had been pleased to hire the older woman, whose daughter, Regina, was a couple of years behind Cici in school. The young woman had died years earlier from breast cancer. She'd been so young—her loss a terrible tragedy for the community. Just months later, Carole's husband had drowned in a hot tub. The rumors that swirled out to Cici claimed he'd been high at the time of his death.

Cici never asked, and Carole never discussed her family.

Cici smiled at her friend and closest work companion. "Of course."

Carole closed the door and leaned against the wooden panel. "Susan Johnson is here," Carole said in a dramatic whisper. "She wants to talk to you."

Cici's eyes widened and something in her expression must have alerted Carole, because the older woman slammed her hands onto the old wooden desk with a vicious *whomp* and leaned in close.

"Breathe, Reverend," she demanded.

Cici nodded and managed to suck much-needed air through her nose. After two more breaths, the black spots in front of Cici's eyes dissipated.

"Does she know I was there yesterday?" Cici managed to ask. "That I found…Donald?"

Carole cocked her head. Her eyes narrowed. "How could she possibly know that? *I* didn't know that."

The unsaid words surrounded by Carole's irritation reverberated around the room: *I should have known.* That's because Carole ferreted out information from pretty much everyone, which made her a fantastic church secretary—as well as a few words Cici preferred not to use.

Cici stood, clenching her teeth as her legs shook. But she needed a moment to walk around her office to clear her head.

"This is Santa Fe. Everyone talks. And I just told you now."

"Susan would have to be asking specific questions to know you found Donald yesterday," Carole said, her voice stiff. She did not like Cici knowing details before her. "Where did you find him, anyway?"

Cici shook out her arms and wiggled her head on her neck. "Oh. Aspen Vista Trail. Sam and I were already hiking it when the call came in. And good point. As always. So. You'll send her in, and we'll see what she knows."

"I'll bring you a latte, too."

"Thanks," Cici said, trying to control her shaking hands. "I need the caffeine."

"Rough night?"

Cici barely heard the words, instead drawn back into the strange feeling she got—and missed so desperately—when Anna Carmen was close. She sent out a feeler, but Anna Carmen refused to answer. Or maybe Cici was fixated on the idea of her sister's image appearing to her yesterday, but it never actually happened. Sam had assumed Cici fell into shock. Maybe he'd been right.

Cici rubbed her palms down her face, wishing for some level of certainty about what happened yesterday. She had none. Not even her daily prayer time this morning eased her riotous emotions.

Carole made a sound of disapproval as she walked over to the door, opened it, and walked down the short office hallway to the reception area.

Cici heard her say, "Reverend Gurule is finishing her call. You can head on back."

What? Oh, right! Donald's wife was coming into her office.

Cici dived toward her office phone, picked it up, and pressed it hard—too hard—to her ear. She dropped her gaze to her desk but peeked up from under her lashes as she made noncommittal noises into the phone. The dial tone caused her headache to pound harder.

Susan entered the room, her eyes puffy and her nose red and raw. The woman's posture was bent inward.

Carole waved to get Cici's attention as she pretended to get off the phone.

"We can discuss those stoles more later. Thanks for the call."

Cici hung up, trying to overcome her grimace. Stoles? Really? Already, she'd failed at this cloak-and-dagger crap.

"I'll get that coffee, Cee. Susan, you want anything?" Carole asked, her hand cupping Susan's shoulder with solicitude.

Susan shook her head.

"Never mind on the coffee, then," Cici said, dropping the phone back into its cradle. She stood and rounded the desk. "Susan. I was deeply sorrowed to hear of Donald's untimely death."

Susan fell into Cici's arms in a fit of tears.

Carole raised her eyebrows even higher as Susan began to bawl, sputtering incomprehensible words in between sobs.

"What was that?" Cici asked, running her hand up and down Susan's back in a soothing gesture.

Susan reared back, her eyes fierce. "Donald was having a blasted affair."

"Er. That's not what I expected." At Carole's rolled eyes, Cici took Susan's hands and led her to the small seating area opposite the desk. "Let's sit here and you can tell me."

Once Susan sat, so did Cici. Carole hovered by the door.

"I was down in Albuquerque this weekend for a conference," Susan began on a sigh.

Easy enough to confirm. Sam would already be looking into it, Cici was sure.

"The call...I was *shocked*. Donald doesn't hike. He has a heart condition."

That was news. "Really?"

"Taking a stroll down our street has been the extent of our physical activity for the past year. So for him to be at the top of a trail…no, nope. Something happened. Or *someone*."

Susan dabbed at her eye with an already-soaked tissue.

"I knew I should have found his lack of interest in me more worrisome, but with menopause…"

Cici shot Carole a panicked look. This interview took a side turn into a place Cici never anticipated.

"Such a challenging time in a marriage," Cici murmured.

Carole smirked, probably because Cici managed to sound normal.

"And to find out some woman posed to be *me* on that phone call. Dammit."

Susan slammed her palm down on the arm of the chair, causing Cici to jump.

"If Donald had to go and get himself killed, the least the rat bastard could do was have the thoughtfulness and dignity to die doing something seemly."

"You have no idea who this woman is?" Cici asked.

Not only did Cici want to know, Sam needed to find the connection to solve Donald's case—and for a chance to solve Anna Carmen's, which remained a painful mystery not just to the two of them, but for the community at large. Anna Carmen Gurule was voted teacher of the year and had many hopeful parents at Capitol High School hoping their child would be taught by the young, enthusiastic woman.

Her death left a huge hole in the community—one Cici desperately sought to fill.

You could help me out here, you know, Cici yelled mentally at her silent twin, her disposition souring.

Nope. Anna Carmen proved her same stubborn self even in death. Anna Carmen made a point to pop in on the mountain yesterday basically in Technicolor, but now refused to come back—even when Cici begged her.

"No idea. How stupid does that make me that I had *no idea* he was cheating?"

Susan's eyes filled with tears once more and she put her face in her hands as she sobbed.

"Thirty-one years together, and it's all over. Not just our life together, but the life I *thought* we had for all those years. All I have to show for it is a shih tzu I can't stand."

And a fat bank account, thanks to Donald's thirty-plus years with one of the most prestigious law firms in the region.

Cici leaned forward and pressed her palms to Susan's, wishing she had more to offer the older woman. A fresh bout of sobs burst out of Susan's trembling mouth. Carole offered a tissue, and Susan used it plus two more before she calmed enough to continue.

"We'll need to have a funeral," Susan muttered.

"Absolutely. If that's what you want, we can do that."

Susan raised her head, eyes burning with hate, but also filled with a deep-seated despair that worried Cici.

"Just don't say anything about Don being a good man. He's obviously a lying, cheating SOB in addition to being a blood-thirsty attorney. He *deserved* what he got up there. Since he's stabbed me straight through the heart."

"Perhaps there is a misunderstanding in here, Susan. Donald seemed to care for you, very much."

Susan stared down at her lap, shredding another tissue. She picked at a sculpted nail and pursed her lips. Then, much to Cici's shock, she leaned forward and held Cici's gaze with a flinty one of her own.

"He seemed to care for his work, too, but after a trip down to Madrid last week, he *quit*."

4

Stars, hide your fires; Let not light see my black and deep desires. — Shakespeare

"He quit?" Cici stuttered.

"He didn't even have the nerve to tell me," Susan wailed. "See? How could I be so stupid about him having an affair? He didn't talk to me about anything important." She jabbed her pointer finger toward Cici. "You tell that young man of yours about Don. He needs to know."

"Who?" Cici reared back, about six follow-up questions ready to spill from her lips.

"That detective," Susan said. "He needs to know. He's going to need to know everything…"

Susan once again collapsed into Cici's arms, shaking there. Many long, wet minutes later, Carole cleared her throat.

Cici jumped. She'd forgotten the secretary had remained in the room with her.

"Come on, Susan. Let me get you home," Carole said, her voice soft. "Come on now. You're beyond exhausted. So much emotion and nothing makes sense."

She clucked as Susan gripped her tissue, shaking. Carole placed her arm around Susan's waist. "Do you have family coming in? Who can I call to help you?" she asked, leading Susan from the room.

Cici returned to her desk, exhaustion grappling with each of her muscles. With a sigh, she picked up her cell phone. She texted Sam.

He called her within minutes. "What's going on, Cee?"

Cici dropped her head forward, letting her aching eyes slide closed. "Like I told you, Susan Johnson just left my office. Sam, she said Donald quit working last week. I don't…that seems weird."

Sam made a grunting noise. "I'm following a lead now." His voice roughened as it always did when he was concerned. "Walk me through your conversation? But, first, where's Susan?"

"Carole took her home."

"You're at the church by yourself?" Definitely a hard edge to Sam's words.

"No. Our pianist and choir are here, practicing. And we have a knitting group in one of the classrooms."

"Don't stay alone, Cee. Promise me."

Cici shivered, once again reliving the beseeching look in her sister's eyes—their desperation for truth but also fear, Cici was sure, for her.

"I won't."

"Okay. Tell me what Susan said. Everything you remember."

Cici launched into a recitation.

Sam remained quiet. "I'm researching Donald's heart problem. I'll get on his sudden retirement, too. I hadn't gotten over to his law firm yet."

"All right."

"Susan told you to tell me about that?"

"Yes."

"Huh."

Sam waited a beat, and Cici bet he was thinking.

"I'll call you later. Make sure you made it home safe."

"Sam," Cici said on a sigh. "I can handle this."

"Not sure I can," Sam mumbled before he disconnected.

Cici spent the next couple of hours welcoming other congregants for their activities and following up with her emails and paperwork. Carole came back and said Susan was resting. Her sister was on a flight that arrived in a couple of hours. Cici jotted down a note reminding her to visit with Susan tomorrow.

By four, the most pressing business of the day was complete, but Cici remained unsettled by her conversation with Susan. She wanted answers—not the additional questions Susan's revelations created.

Linda Yoder stopped in to let Cici know the knitting group was leaving.

"You look wrung out," the older woman said with concern. "Need anything?"

"No," Cici said, finding her first smile of the afternoon. "I'll feel better once I clear my head. But thank you for asking."

"All right. Well, see you next week." Linda waved, trotting off at a fast clip, her knitting needles clacking together in her large canvas tote.

Cici stood and stretched, her words to Linda revolving in her mind.

She went home to her large fur babies, Rodolfo circling her legs and licking her ankles. Cici pet both him and his sister, Mona. Cici walked them a couple of miles before feeding them dinner. Still unsettled by the last couple of days, Cici stared at her garage.

Sometimes, the best course of action is to take a deep breath and take a ride.

Cici strapped on her helmet, and patted the handlebars of her vintage 1965 Electra Glide Harley she inherited from Anna Carmen.

The electric-blue motorcycle had sat in her garage for the better part of the last fifteen months, driven just far enough to keep all the mechanics well-lubricated and in top working order.

That changed today.

Cici shoved the key in the ignition and headed south on Saint Francis. She let out a whoop of sheer joy at the freedom of riding the bike. After a few harrowing miles, braving both the nutty locals and the confused tourists on I-25, Cici exited onto NM-14 where she turned south again for a ride down the scenic highway that led to the small artsy town of Madrid—a popular tourist destination even though it only boasted a handful of shops and restaurants on its one main drag.

Oh, how she loved the vibrations up her arms, the wind streaming over her body, the low growl of the engine. Anna Carmen always said there was nothing like riding her hog.

Cici smiled inside her helmet.

"You got that right," she said with a soft, heartfelt sigh. "Miss you, sis."

The late summer sun cast a golden haze over the foothills, spilling across the road and warming Cici's back, almost as if her sister was offering a heavenly hug.

Cici's breath hitched with bittersweet memories as she pulled into the parking lot of the little café she liked, its red umbrellas shading much of the patio. She pocketed her keys and pulled the leather gloves from her hands. After setting her helmet in its place, she combed her fingers through her long, wind-blown hair.

"Hey, RG! What's your pleasure today?" asked Jaycee, the bright, bubbly teenager who acted both as hostess and head waitress. She was in her senior year at Saint Michael's, a cheerleader and all-around awesome young woman—and the girl dating Juanito Sanchez, much to old Mrs. Sanchez's chagrin. Cici was glad she was part of the youth congregation at her church.

"Blessings, Jaycee. I wish you'd call me Cici. Everyone else does."

Jaycee rolled her brown eyes. "Uh-uh. My mom would kill me, seeing as how you're our preacher and all."

"Reverend," Cici replied, her shoulders drooping a bit. Not that the semantics mattered that much, but still. She'd worked hard for her degree—spending years of her life steeped in the Bible, Greek, Latin, and too many philosophical debates.

After some serious soul-searching at Anna Carmen's funeral and during the ensuing weeks, Cici had broken off her already tenuous relationship with Lyndon and moved home with a grief-laden heart to take over the church her sister had begged her to head.

Maybe, Cici often wondered, if she'd accepted the position sooner, Anna Carmen wouldn't be dead. Maybe, if Cici had focused more on her own family instead of chasing silly dreams of trips to South America, she'd be riding down NM-14 with her sister next to her, not just wishing she were there.

The burden of grief caused her stomach to roil and her head to pound.

"Something soothing?" Jaycee asked, eyeing her with concern. "Chamomile?"

"Yes. That's perfect. Thank you."

Cici settled into one of the metal chairs. She laid her gloves on the table and tipped her head back to stare at the red awning overhead.

"Mom said you're doing Mr. Johnson's funeral on Saturday," Jaycee said. She rested her hand on the back of Cici's chair. "The tea's steeping."

"Yes. That's what his wife wanted. How'd you hear that?"

"Email prayer chain."

"Ah," Cici said with a nod.

Carole, always efficient, must have sent that message before she shuttered the church for the evening. "We'll make it happen."

"I'll miss Mr. Johnson," Jaycee said. "He stopped in here about once a week."

Cici knit her brows. "He did? Why?"

Jaycee shrugged. "I never asked. But he stopped by at least once a week for coffee and apple pie."

Cici wondered if Susan knew about this proclivity of Donald's. What on God's green earth had the man been doing in Madrid? His office was near the Plaza. Madrid was a good twenty-five, maybe thirty minutes from there.

"Sit tight," Jaycee said. "I'll bring out your tea with a scone."

"Thanks, but I don't need the scone." Cici was fit—walking

two large young dogs kept her that way for the most part. But Cici only stood five-foot-five, meaning that with each passing year, she had to watch her carb intake with greater care.

"They're fresh. Right out of the oven," Jaycee said in a coaxing voice.

"Bring me two," Cici said.

Baked goods were her weakness. Well, one of her weaknesses. The other was craft beer, specifically local microbrews that she blamed Sam for introducing her to.

Thankfully, her congregation, who already knew to bribe her with cookies and muffins, did not know of her penchant for beer. And Cici planned to keep that secret as long as she could.

Offering the sermon at Donald's funeral this weekend held no appeal, especially now that Cici must wonder if this was where Don met that lover of his. Cici sighed, hating how her thoughts twisted, becoming as bitter as Susan's were earlier.

"You're thinking awful hard."

Cici's lips quirked upward. "Sam. Do you use your badge to stalk me?"

"Don't need to. Jaycee called. Said you looked down."

Sam slid into the chair next to her. His eyes stroked over her face and for the first time all day, Cici began to relax.

"I've been here all of ten minutes. Did you drive with your lights on?"

"I was in Madrid, picking up a gift. I'd waved to Jaycee when I passed the restaurant earlier."

Cici wrinkled her nose. "Please tell me it's not for Jeannette."

Sam tipped back his chair and crossed his arms. "I won't."

Cici shook her head. Jeannette was Sam's on-and-off girl-friend. They'd met about a year ago when she began working as the mayor's executive assistant. Apparently, she was on again, which meant Sam was going to go MIA for a few weeks, only to call Cici to go to the bar, where Cici would drag him home, drunker than a tourist hitting the local brewpubs.

She'd have to stay the night in his guestroom on that lumpy, musty futon she despised. If the last few times proved true, Sam would spend the next week sulking before they could finally get back to their weekly hikes and easy camaraderie.

Jaycee set her large cup of tea and the pot in front of Cici, along with a white paper sack. Cici smiled her thanks and turned back to Sam, who eyed her tea with suspicion.

"Tea?"

"I'm tired, heartsore, and on Anna Carmen's bike."

"The bike, huh? I wondered when I saw it out front." Sam swallowed and nodded. "I'll have tea, too," he said to Jaycee. "But the iced version."

Jaycee bobbed her head and darted off.

Cici rolled her head along the back of the chair. "Why?"

"Why am I with Jeannette?"

No, that wasn't what Cici was thinking, but she was curious, so she kept her mouth shut.

Sam stared at the bustling sidewalk across the street. Tour-ists, laden with shopping bags and cameras, jostled their way in and out of the glassblowing gallery and other small art studios. From this angle, his blue eyes were opaque—a strange black. Cici shifted in her chair and Sam turned back toward her.

"Because I can't have the woman I want."

Cici closed her eyes as tears pressed against the lids and burned into her nose.

Sam brought his chair down with a soft thump as it hit the patio paver but he didn't say anything for another long moment.

"Anna Carmen was my best friend. She helped me through a hard time—she helped me see what I couldn't then."

Cici's lip trembled as she lifted her teacup. "I miss her, too. So much. Yesterday…it all came bubbling back up."

Sam's hand settled on Cici's shoulder in that gesture of comfort she'd come to depend on.

"I know you do. And, yeah, I figured it would."

Jaycee sidled up to their table and settled Sam's large glass of iced tea on the table. Condensation formed on the glass, dripping down to wet the white napkin beneath it.

"I thought of something," the girl said.

Both Cici and Sam turned their faces up to the teenager.

"Mr. Johnson told me one time he was meeting someone about a case." Her brow wrinkled for a moment before she shrugged. "Does that help?"

Sam tugged at his short ponytail. "Maybe. Thanks, Jaycee."

"Sure." The girl skittered off to greet some new patrons.

"You think you know what the case is, don't you?" Cici asked, pouring more tea into her cup.

"Cici, I wasn't in the area for Jeannette," Sam said, ignoring the question at hand. Sam's words jolted through Cici—mostly because of the tone. He used his all-business one that caused her to straighten in her seat. "Though I probably should get her something, seeing as how she's my date Friday for the city shindig."

Cici sipped her tea, ignoring the heat biting into her tongue. The taste rolled down her throat, easing into her nauseous belly.

"Oh?"

"I came here to dig into the lead about Don I'd mentioned earlier." Sam paused, seeming uncertain. Very un-Sam-like. The nausea in Cici's stomach slammed back even stronger. She set the teacup farther from her.

"See, I got word of an opioid ring down this way. It's outside of my jurisdiction, but I wanted to talk to the county sheriff about it."

"Why?"

"For a few reasons. I think Donald was helping the DEA flush out the opioid prescriber."

Cici picked up her teacup but then immediately set it back in the saucer, her eyes never leaving Sam's face.

"Hold up. You think Donald Johnson—the big shot lawyer— was popping 'Contin?"

Sam leaned forward, lacing his fingers together as he lay them on the table. "I didn't say that. But maybe. I don't know."

He let out an exasperated grunt, his biceps flexing as he gripped his chair.

"After my talk with the local guys here today, I know Donald drove down to the Madrid post office to pick up a stash of something. His PO box has opioids in it. Or did. They were confiscated about an hour ago. Evidence."

Cici leaned back in her chair, her mouth unhinged. She

managed to snap it shut with a shake of her head.

"No. Way."

Sam lifted his glass and drank deep.

"I mean, I believe you," Cici said. "But that's…Donald was so integral to the community. He donated to all the arts. Heck, he was at The Lensic gala in March!"

"Wealth doesn't mean you don't have problems, Cee. Think of your parents," Sam said gently.

Cici picked up her teacup again and drained the now-tepid liquid. "Right. I just need to wrap my head around Donald being an opioid-addict."

Sam tapped his blunt-edged index finger on the top of his glass.

"I think Madrid's drug ring is connected to the bigger one up in Santa Fe," he said. "We haven't been brought in on any investigation there, but…" He faltered.

"Are you supposed to be telling me this?" Cici asked, suspicious. Sam held everything close—words, emotions, definitely work.

His lips compressed before he met her gaze. His pale eyes seemed like shards of glass. Nothing good. Whatever he was about to tell her, Cici wouldn't like.

"No, I'm not."

Her hands began to shake just like they did whenever Anna Carmen's name was about to pop into a conversation. She just… well, this must be part of the twin thing. Cici felt her sister's name sliding into the conversation before it did.

"What's going on, Sam? Wait," she said. Cici frowned, sidetracked by a tidbit, latching on to it, trying to breathe through a certainty she would never be able to change. "You're telling me this all happens through the mail?"

Sam took a deep drink through his straw as he lifted his eyebrow.

"I don't know why I'm surprised," Cici murmured. She poured herself another cup of tea, sipped as she tried to find some modicum of control. *Oh, Anna Carmen, what did you do?* "It's just…mail seems so passé."

Sam set his drink down. "Probably why it's worked. Gotta have a physical drop for the drugs, and it's safer than having people meet on street corners."

He played with his straw for another moment, then blew out a breath.

"I actually planned to see you later tonight."

Cici leaned forward. This was it. What she didn't want to hear. Sam turned to face her, his mouth twisting as if the words he was about to say settled sour in his mouth.

"The drug business," he said. "In Santa Fe."

Cici nodded encouragement even though she wanted to stand, to scream, to run away. Anything to keep Sam from uttering the next words.

Sam blew out a breath. "I've known this for a while, but I didn't want to tell you."

"Spit it out, Sam. Now that you started, I need to hear the rest."

His eyes smiled but his mouth remained pressed flat. His lawyer face, Cici called it. That ability to keep his facial muscles relaxed was better than any poker player's she'd seen. That's what made him such a great detective—that's why he'd been chosen for that special task force in Denver. But Anna Carmen's death changed Sam's life nearly as dramatically as it changed Cici's.

And what continued to connect them—the loss of the one person who could impact both their past and future.

"It's moved around a bit. Started in Santa Fe, and I'm sure it's the same one that's here. The MO is the same, anyway."

Cici blinked out of her haze and focused on Sam's words.

"The drug cartel thingy?" Her heart rate sped up even further. No. No way Anna Carmen was linked to drugs.

This time, Sam did smile even as he shook his head. Yeah, Cici knew she had a way with words.

"It started on the university campus," he murmured.

"Saint John's?" Cici gasped. That's where Anna Carmen attended just about ten years ago now—so she could live at home and help their ailing mother, who'd passed away just weeks into their senior year of college.

Anna Carmen won the better all-around human award compared to Cici. Not that it did her much good. Cici was still here and Anna Carmen was lying in her coffin.

"Nah. Art and Design."

Cici dropped her chin to her chest, relief flooding her system. Donald's death, Anna Carmen's appearance on the mountain yesterday, clearly turned Cici's mind to mush. She was attempting to make connections to her sister where none existed.

"Yeah. Okay."

Sam finished his tea and pushed the glass away. "But this does have to do with Anna Carmen."

Crud. She'd just talked herself out of her sister's involvement. Cici also pushed away her teacup again, her stomach too knotted to hold anything further—even something as soothing as chamomile.

Sam once again faced the street, apparently unable to meet her eyes.

"As you and I already guessed and the Office of Medical Investigation confirmed about an hour ago, the same type of knife was used to strike Donald. A switch blade. In the same location as Anna Carmen—the kidney. We've seen one other death like that in the past few years. Also unsolved."

He paused, waiting for Cici to digest this information. Cici dipped her head, eyes wide and fixed on Sam's face.

"And if we infer that Donald's killer is the same as Anna Carmen's, which we'll definitely pursue, then we need to go back and look at the drug trafficking ring at Santa Fe College to determine if there's a link there between the killer and Anna Carmen. Because we know Anna Carmen knew Donald through your father. The net's tightening on this whole investigation."

Cici's chair scraped a harsh shriek as she shoved back from the table. Sam didn't turn back toward her, probably because he knew what was coming next.

"Screw you, Sam."

He didn't even flinch as she snarled the words.

"And screw your shitty investigation that would try to link my sister to some drug ring."

He didn't move as she picked up her gloves and stormed from the café.

5

Though this be madness, yet there is method in't.
— Shakespeare

Anna Carmen dealing drugs—taking drugs—was like…like Cici dealing drugs. She snorted.

Anathema.

That's what it was! Anna Carmen helped children get an education. She didn't slide dope under desks to children. The idea was ludicrous.

Cici slammed the door to her house, her mood even blacker now that she'd had time to further process Sam's accusations about her twin. That *he*—the man who seemed to adore Anna Carmen for so much of their lives—would make the accusations that Anna Carmen had been involved in something nefarious, cut deep.

Near as deep as losing her sister.

And, knowing Sam as well as she did, Cici knew *he* knew that. Which was what made the revelation hurt even more. Because Sam never would have told her if he didn't have some evidence— something concrete—to prove Anna Carmen's involvement with a drug ring.

Rodolfo and Mona danced around Cici, nuzzling into her hand and whining low in their throats. Cici dropped to her knees and flung her arms around Rodolfo, the larger of the two Great Pyrenees. Mona pressed her warm shoulder into Cici's back and licked her ear.

"I'll be okay. Just…give me a minute."

She talked to her dogs. So what? Cici lived alone—it wasn't like there were other people around for a constant high brown conversation. Plus, her dogs never told her terrible truths.

Even if she needed to hear them.

Cici sighed into Rodolfo's thick white fur before she sat back.

"You two need to potty? How about another short walk?"

She came home from their trip around the block to find a white paper sack with her scones and a bouquet of hyacinth, her favorite flower, on the porch chair next to her front door. No note, not that she needed one.

She didn't smile when she shoved her nose into the soft, sweet blooms, but the headache that pounded against her temples all day receded a bit.

———

A few hours later, Cici shoved back from her computer, rubbing her eyes. Her sermon remained nothing more than the weekly liturgical reading. Words wouldn't come.

Cici continued to see her sister's hazel eyes staring back at her. Her eyes, too, but Anna Carmen's always seemed so full of life, of goodness.

Her phone rang again—for the tenth time that night.

Not Sam. He'd wait for her to call him. She needed to…
to thank him for the flowers. She hesitated once again. He was probably with Jeannette by now anyway.

After changing into her pajamas and brushing her teeth, Cici climbed into bed with a sigh. Her body ached from fatigue but also from guilt. Sam told her about Anna Carmen because he wanted her to be prepared for the news hitting not just the papers but the gossipmongers' tongues. They'd prove more vicious to both Cici and her extended family than the paper or even Anna Carmen's former students and families, all of whom adored Anna Carmen and probably wouldn't believe she'd been involved in something so sordid as drugs.

Cici couldn't believe that herself. Not that Sam said Anna Carmen was involved in *selling* drugs. Thank God.

"You better not have been, Aci," Cici said. "Or I'd be likely to stomp on your grave."

She thumbed off a quick text, letting Sam know she appreciated the scones, the flowers, and the heads-up on Anna Carmen's name popping back up now that details of Donald Johnson's death would begin to make the rounds.

At least now, maybe, she would sleep. Rodolfo and Mona assumed their positions on their large pillows next to her bed. Cici pet Mona's ears absently, thinking about Lyndon. He now oversaw that large dig in South America, in the location they'd chosen together. She'd also heard that he'd married two months ago, and if alumni gossip was to be believed (it was—those people knew things), he and his lovely blond bride were expecting their first child early in the new year.

When she'd told Lyndon goodbye, Cici had sworn off intimate relationships. That had been the right choice then.

But now? Cici was lonely.

Sad and lonely and not at all healed in her soul. Even after all this time.

Her dogs were the last descendants she had found that were born from Anna Carmen's Great Pyrenees. In fact, these two were the children of Anna Carmen's dog, Gidget. When these two passed, Cici would lose her last living, breathing connection to her sister.

"I miss you, Aci. I wish I understood better what you'd been going through."

She swallowed hard and tilted her head back to stare at her beamed ceiling. "We weren't as good as I projected, but maybe I shouldn't have pushed Lyndon away when he tried to help me through losing you."

Cici blinked, then swiped at the lone tear sliding down her cheek.

"I wish I wasn't alone. Even though I know it's all my own fault."

And, for the first time since the moment on the mountain, she felt her sister's presence. Almost as if Anna Carmen wrapped her in a hug. Cici's breathing evened out and she slid into slumber.

The dream was tinged in blood.

Anna Carmen's blood.

"You should have stopped pushing when you received the letter." The voice whispered low and vicious in her ear, causing Cici to shiver. The voice sounded deeper than most females' but not the low baritone of many of the males Anna Carmen knew. Hard to place, possibly on purpose. A faint, familiar scent wafted toward her face as people milled around. Such a large crowd this year. No one noticed the person pressed close to Anna Carmen's back.

"Powerful people want you to stop fishing for information. Don told you, too. I saw you talking to him. You should have listened."

No one turned toward her when she bowed back as a searing pain unlike anything she'd ever felt before ripped her ability to breathe, to scream, to stand.

Anna Carmen's hand—well, Cici's hand in the dream—came away from her side covered in blood. Anna Carmen, no…*Cici* as Anna Carmen, turned even as she sank to her knees. Someone screamed. Another scream. People rushing toward her. Too late, she wanted to say, but couldn't. Her vision dimmed.

She tried to breathe through the searing pain in her side and back. She tried to see who had hurt her.

Someone's back, clad in a leather duster long enough to form an androgynous shape. Hair hidden under a beige felt cowboy hat. A quail feather stuck out at a jaunty angle.

Cici. She'll be hurt by my death. And Evan.

The man Anna Carmen planned to marry. Evan should be here. No, Anna Carmen *shouldn't* be here. She should be with Evan at La Casa Sena, drinking some nice wine on the patio.

She never needed to get involved. She should have backed off when she received the first note.

Oh, Evan, you were right. I'm so, so sorry.

Cici awoke with a great shuddering start. Both dogs stood at attention next to her, quivering.

She must have screamed. She sat up, rubbing her palms over her sweaty face.

"Oh, Anna Carmen. *What* did you involve me in?"

6

The fault, dear Brutus, is not in our stars,
but in ourselves. — Shakespeare

Donald Johnson's funeral proved a nice, if staid, affair, thanks in large part to Carole's amazing organizational skills. Cici met with Susan once more in person and the two spoke again on the phone so that Cici could gather the information she needed to give Donald the send-off he deserved.

Carole handled the pianist and flowers. She'd worked with Susan to get together a guest list and confirm timing with the caterers who'd set up for the wake at the Johnsons' large home off Canyon Road, not too far from the oldest galleries and some of the best eateries in town.

Cici had already begged off the fancy evening, claiming she needed to work on her sermon, which she did.

More, she wanted to avoid seeing many of her father's old colleagues, who would, no doubt, ask how he was.

Cici didn't know.

Didn't *want* to know.

Susan sat in the front pew, stiff and dry-eyed, next to her younger sister. Donald and she had no children and neither had large extended families, meaning many of the mourners were friends and colleagues.

How had Susan not realized Donald had a drug problem?

How did any couple live together and not realize the other party was keeping some monumental secret? Like, in her parents' case, a long-standing affair.

Cici took a deep breath and refocused on her notes settled on the podium in front of her.

If Cici hadn't spoken with Susan so often this week, she'd think the older woman's shock related to Donald's murder. Instead, Susan ached for the last earthly betrayals Donald perpetrated.

No one knew anything about the woman who called in Donald's location.

The phone number used was from a burner phone they'd found—wiped clean both of prints and of data—in the possession of one of the homeless men the police picked up weekly from the Plaza.

Cici spotted Sam sitting toward the back of her sanctuary. Jeannette sat next to him, as polished and sophisticated as her position as executive assistant to the mayor dictated. Her light, glossy hair was pulled back in a neat chignon and her suit must have been custom-tailored to fit her five-foot-nine form. She leaned in close and whispered something in Sam's ear. Cici brought her gaze back to the mourners nearer the front. J.R. Pattison III and his wife, Joan, sat front and center. Joan's eyes were as warm as always, though J.R. seemed distracted. Perhaps he was considering his workload as the sole remaining partner in the law firm where Donald worked.

Cici inhaled sharply through her nose, letting the air trickle slowly back out. She stepped up to the microphone at the lectern in front of the congregation. Her throat was dry but she ignored her physical discomfort.

"Thank you for coming today to help us celebrate the life of Donald Johnson."

———

Cici finished the service with her standard benediction, her hand held up to include everyone in the room, before heading over to embrace Susan.

"That was beautiful," Susan murmured in a low voice. She patted Cici's white robe, adjusting the deep purple stole Cici wore over her vestments. "Too bad the ass didn't deserve such a moving tribute."

Cici squeezed Susan's finger with gentle pressure. "Any time you want to talk, call me. Or Carole. We'll be here for you during this difficult time."

Susan snorted.

"I'm heading to Cabo for a month, maybe longer," she said. "I always wanted to go, but Don was too busy with work. Good thing he left me a nice fat retirement plan to help me get over him. With a cabana boy or a beach bum."

Cici walked Susan out of the sanctuary, keeping her arm around the older woman, even though Susan appeared more than capable of walking on her own. Others began to trickle out, some to shake Susan's hand and express their sympathies, others to give Cici an earful about her ceremony.

For the most part, the feedback was positive. Only Mrs. Hodgkins complained about the piano concertos chosen. Donna, the church's pianist—who held a master's degree in music theory from Juilliard—rolled her eyes discreetly, causing Cici to cover her laugh with an abrupt cough.

Donna smirked as she whispered her goodbyes to Cici, then promised more loudly to be in extra early tomorrow to work on her music. Mrs. Hodgkins nodded, telling Donna she really needed the practice. She hobbled off toward the small shuttle her retirement community sent for her.

Sam strolled up to Cici, hands in his suit pockets.

"Did good up there, slugger."

"Not my first rodeo, cowboy."

Sam smirked but his eyes continued to study her face. "I hurt you the other day."

Cici dipped her head to the side. No point in denying it.

"Thanks for coming," she said. "Though, I'm guessing it was more related to work than to support the reverend."

"Oh, I don't know," Sam said, rocking back on his heels. "Could be a bit of both."

"Discover anything useful?" Cici asked.

Jeannette joined them, curving her arm through Sam's and tugging him closer to her side. "Cecilia. Lovely service. But then, all your services are amazing."

Cici smiled. "Blessings, Jeannette. Thank you for coming today. How is your family? Didn't I hear something about a sick father?"

Jeannette tucked a loose strand of hair behind her ear, her gaze darting up to Sam's face before returning to Cici.

"Good. Yeah, I went home for a week to see him. He's better now. Thanks for asking."

"How did you know Donald?" Cici asked.

Her smiled pulled, straining at the edges.

"Oh, um. He stopped in the mayor's office a couple times a month. We liked Donald. He always brought us in pastries from Clafouti's. That man remembered my love of peach preserves and made sure there was always a jar of the stuff in with the croissants."

Jeannette shook her head, her eyes a bit damp. "With all Don had going on, he remembered something as silly as my favorite jelly."

Sam looked startled. "I didn't realize you knew him well."

Jeannette pursed her lips. "*Well* is an overstatement."

She straightened her suit jacket, dusted a piece of lint from her sleeve.

"But he treated the mayor's staff like we were humans. One of the few who came in regularly who even knew our names, really. And he always enjoyed talking to me about his pro bono work that he did for the local nonprofits."

Cici caught Sam's eye, and he dipped his head. He'd pursue Donald's relationship with Jeannette and the mayor as soon as he had the chance. Other people pressed forward, forcing Sam and Jeannette to move along.

But like her, Sam now wondered if Jeannette and Don had spent more time together...say in a romantic fashion. Cici shifted her weight, sending up a prayer that Jeannette wasn't Don's mistress. And not just for Sam's sake. That would be...awkward to try to explain to Susan.

Cici shook hands with another seventy or so people. Donald's legal work, both with the city's elite and the nonprofits, made him popular with the art and scientific community, leading to an eclectic mix of attendees.

"Cee. Good to see you."

Evan Reynolds, Anna Carmen's last boyfriend, patted Cici awkwardly on the shoulder. Remembering her dream and the feeling that something was off with Evan—that's why Anna Carmen wasn't with him that afternoon she died—caused Cici to remain wooden.

He pulled back and settled his hands on Cici's shoulders, studying her face. Probably wondering if she was still angry with him for the last words they'd exchanged.

She was.

She wouldn't ever get past the cruelty of his words—no one called her sister a whore.

"Sometimes, it's so hard to see you," Evan said.

Cici closed her eyes against the pain of that statement. It wasn't as if she'd chosen to be Anna Carmen's identical twin. Not that she'd change her years or relationship with her sister. She never would—unless it was to make their bond stronger, last longer.

Maybe Evan understood he'd hurt her because he said, "You look beautiful. But then, you always did. Do."

Cici forced a smile. "Thank you for coming to the service, Evan. I didn't realize you were friendly with Donald."

Evan 's smile fell. "Not really friendly. We—ah—knocked skulls a few times. At work."

Evan focused mainly on bankruptcies. Considering the first groups to get shafted out of money tended to be the nonprofits Donald championed, Cici could understand the tension. And that might explain why the two men never seemed particularly happy to be in the same room together.

"And speaking of that…" Evan glanced around before leaning in closer. "Anna Carmen met with Donald before she died."

Everything inside her stopped for a long beat. "What?"

"I'm just saying there's a reason they were both stabbed to death."

Cici shivered. "You know about his stabbing? That it's like… how?"

"I asked."

Evan threw his chin toward Sam, whose narrowed eyes remained focused on Cici.

"Sam didn't want to play nice, but he knew I'd go over his head."

He leaned in closer, his voice lowering. "Whatever Anna Carmen got herself involved in, it's not over. Don't get sucked in, too."

"Reverend?" Carole appeared at Cici's elbow. Cici turned toward her, hoping the fear wasn't visible all over her face.

"Donald's family wanted a word. You'll excuse us, won't you?" Carole turned a guileless gaze on Evan, who dipped his head before walking away. He didn't look back. Then again, he hadn't looked back as he walked away from her sister's grave. Why would this experience be any different?

"Hitting on you in your robes," Carole muttered as she pulled Cici through the thinning crowd. "Does no one understand how wrong that is? What is it with young people these days?"

Cici was too stunned by Evan's words to clarify. But when

Carole turned to look at her expectantly, Cici said, "Considering the fact I'm thirty, I don't really think I qualify as a young person."

She pressed a hand to her stomach, over the slick synthetic fabric of her vestment. The conversation—warning—with Evan left her unsettled. She'd untuck her emotions, his words later, try to decipher why her body went so cold and still.

Carole took off Cici's stole, folded it, and stored it in the closet with the others.

"Well you aren't sixty-two, so count your blessings."

"Did you really need me to talk to Donald's family?" Cici asked, shaking off the unease from Evan's words with difficulty.

"No. They've mostly left. Stiff bunch. Old money, I could tell. What did Sam want?" Carole asked as she closed Cici's office door behind them.

"To gauge the crowd, I guess. I didn't talk to him long. Jeannette came over."

Carole's scowl deepened, as it always did when Cici mentioned Jeannette. Cici had no idea what grudge Carole had against the woman, and she didn't plan to ask. She already carried too many secrets in her head to bother with another unsolicited one.

"Right. Well, if we're done here, I'm going to head out. I have to meet Jenny Timkins."

Carole taught archery to students for close to thirty years, one of her hobbies that she increased after her daughter's death.

"How's her training coming along?" Cici asked.

Carole shook her head. "These kids. I don't know how they

talk their parents into thinking they have Olympic-level capabilities. That girl can barely hit the target."

———

Cici locked up the front door to the sanctuary an hour later, glad for the opportunity to finally process Evan's warning. She'd driven her Subaru to the church today—as she did most days. A reverend on a Harley proved more than most people could handle, especially for a funeral.

Good. There was still enough light this afternoon to walk her dogs. She needed a physical outlet for the pent-up energy tugging at her muscles.

The plethora of small bits of gravel and debris crunched under Cici's feet as she approached her car in its accustomed place under the large piñon. She stopped, her hand to her mouth as her keys slid from her other hand to jangle in merry discord on their descent.

Not one, but two dead birds. White birds, too large to be doves, lay on her windshield, blood from their slit throats still dripping onto their once-pristine feathers.

7

To weep is to make less the depth of grief.
— *Shakespeare*

Cici scooped up her keys, her gaze locked with the sharp black eye of the dead bird. Just last week, she'd discovered that a group of crows was called a murder. She had a murder on her windshield.

Aimed at her.

She intended to run back toward the dubious sanctuary of her church, phone already clutched in her other hand. She stumbled back after she slammed into a thick slab of muscle. Her heart pumped hard, begging her to let it continue to do so as a scream built in her throat.

"An omen," Big Joe Benally said, steadying Cici, whose knees had seemed to liquefy as she tipped downward.

"Joe," Cici managed to gasp, "I sure wish you'd arrived fifteen minutes earlier."

"Not my time now," he said. "You pay me to be here for weddings and funerals and from eleven to two every Sunday."

True. And Jim never did anything without much for thought and without it in writing. Though, why he was here now Cici also didn't know.

"I drove by." Jim pointed to the open door of his beat-up

Altima about two steps from where Cici stood. Her heart warmed as she realized he'd stopped after seeing her expression.

"When you drove by, did you see who did this?"

Joe shrugged. "I didn't see anyone. The person didn't want to get caught."

"What does this mean? The omen, I mean." Cici's words came out half-gasped as she gestured toward her car.

Joe squinted his rheumy eyes. While Joe wasn't old—only in his mid-fifties—he'd had many health issues and his eyesight began to fail a few years ago in part due to his untreated diabetes. Now, both his diabetes and his eyes were managed, and he worked security for Cici's church and for a few other places Cici helped set him up with.

"I've only ever heard them spoken of in dreams. There, such beautiful specimens mean aspirations, goals. To see them slaughtered…"

Big Joe shook his head, his chin lowered to his chest. A strange, growly rumble emitted from his chest.

"Nothing good," he muttered.

———

"White ravens are rare," Sam said, looking up at Cici over his mug of tea. Not that he drank any of the steaming liquid. He didn't enjoy hot tea, but Cici was too frazzled after the dead birds to offer him coffee.

"Okay," she said on an expulsion of air. The tension didn't leave her shoulders—or the area behind her breast bone. "So, they're ravens not crows. Are you sure?"

"Um, no. I'm not a bird expert. Does it matter?"

Cici tugged her long, dark hair up into a haphazard bun on the top of her head. "Probably not. Maybe." She shrugged. "A group of crows is called a murder. I just...a murder on my windshield." Cici hugged her arms, running her palms up and down in quick strokes.

"Huh," Sam said. "I had no idea."

He pulled out his phone and typed something into it. "A group of ravens is a conspiracy. That's bad but not as scary as the murder of crows." He typed some more. "Yeah...there are white crows and ravens. Different species. Have black eyes so not albinos."

"Sam?" Cici said, leaning forward. "I'm sure that's all fascinating. But someone sliced the throats of two defenseless creatures this afternoon and left them on the hood of my car. Can we focus on that, please?"

Sam shoved his phone back into his pocket. "Sorry, Cee. I agree someone had to search those suckers out. Finding two would be even more time-consuming. Someone wants you to understand how serious they are."

Cici set her mug on her desk. "It's a statement. I get it. The symbolism Big Joe spoke of. All of it. What I don't get is who or why. Why *now*?"

She picked back up her mug, ignored her shaking hands, and managed to gulp down some of the scalding liquid. She sighed, steadier, as she lowered the cup.

"The whole town now knows you were on the SAR team that found Don. Your sister's death still isn't solved. And someone doesn't want it to be solved."

"Two white crows, murdered. Two innocent people, murdered." She met Sam's concerned blue eyes. "We can assume they're for Aci…I mean Anna Carmen and Donald."

Sam dipped his head in acknowledgment. "Good guess. But that's all it is right now. A guess. Much as I'd like to move on someone, I don't have enough evidence."

"Evan spoke to me. Said Anna Carmen met with Donald not long before her death."

Sam ran his hand over the short spikes of hair across the back of his head. "I knew that. Evan and Anna Carmen fought after that meeting. That's why Anna Carmen was up in Chimayó without Evan that day."

Cici stood and began to pace. She refused to look out the window into the parking lot where the forensics team finished its work.

"Or it's his convenient excuse to explain why he wasn't with my sister when she needed him."

"I don't think so. They were solid. Looked like they were headed toward marriage. We all thought so."

The image of her sister in a bridal gown and veil slid through Cici's mind, causing the ache in her chest to intensify. She'd never see that. Never stand next to her sister again, let alone help her prepare for her wedding. Or hold her sister's child. Call her at Thanksgiving.

The grief of loss ripped through Cici's chest, leaving her raw and edgy.

She turned back toward Sam. "I felt her up on Aspen Ridge. Anna Carmen. She's trying to tell me things."

"Cee," Sam said as he stood.

"She wants me to help you solve Donald's murder. She knows its related to her own."

Sam's mouth trembled a little as he said, "I know you miss Anna Carmen. I do, too. But she's *dead*. And the dead don't talk."

Cici cringed. She'd thought Sam, of all people, would understand. In some ways, she couldn't wrap her head around the fact her twin reached out to her last week.

He opened his mouth to say something else, but Cici raised her hand.

"Don't placate me," she said, her voice sharp. "I don't need it."

She might not be able to explain to Sam, an only child and nonbeliever of anything he couldn't touch or see. Talk about the Doubting Thomas.

What Sam forgot was Anna Carmen was not just her sister. Anna Carmen was her *identical twin*. They shared something much more special than a sibling bond...the *same* DNA.

Something, Cici now believed, not even death could eliminate completely.

"I'm sorry I ruined your plans tonight," she said, unwilling to discuss her conclusions further. "I'm sure Jeannette isn't happy with me."

Sam shrugged as he leaned back in the chair.

"Duty calls. And you know I'll always be around to help you out, Cee."

"You shouldn't have to. And I'm not asking you to believe me about Anna Carmen. I'm telling you, flat-out, I *must* be involved in this. To the bitter end."

Cici shoved her hands into the pockets of her dress slacks, needing something to warm her cold hands. A fist tapped on the office door, cutting off whatever Sam's reply would've been. Cici waved in Justin Espinoza, the forensic photographer, and another member of her church. His gaze lit on Cici, and he scanned her, much as Sam had done, checking to make sure she was unharmed.

"Got what we could out there," Justin said to Sam, turning to shake his hand. He turned back to Cici. "No one broached the locks, so now that we've scoured every inch of your vehicle, you should be good to go."

Justin pulled Cici into a side hug, and because she was tired and scared and heartsick over Sam's lack of faith in her announcement, she went willingly, leaning against Justin's broad shoulder with a sigh. Justin was the high school running back, but over the last few years, he'd given up his rigorous workouts, claiming sprints and even weight lifting hurt his knees.

When he lost his college scholarship to NMSU in his sophomore year—something to do with partying and poor decision-making with booze—Justin bounced around for a few years, taking up photography sometime during that period. He was hired as the forensic photographer by the police chief—and a family friend—and seemed to be doing well now, even if he was once again single. At least, that's what Carole, a distant relative of Justin's through marriage, told Cici a few months ago.

"Thank you, Justin. But I'm not going to drive my car again. At least not tonight. Not until it's cleaned. And blessed or something."

Cici shuddered even as she huddled closer into Justin's

embrace. She'd have to read up on removing bad energy. No way she'd drive her car until she managed to remove all traces of negativity from it.

"I'll get you home, Cee," Justin said. He squeezed her arm one more time before running his palm up and down her biceps. "No worries."

"I'll be ready in a moment," Cici said, collecting the mugs from her desk.

After dumping out Sam's full cup of tea and setting them both in the sink, Cici walked back to her office to retrieve her purse and keys. Justin helped her slide into her coat, though it was still warm enough she didn't need it. Sam stayed by her other side as they walked out the door. Both men waited for her to set the alarm and lock up before Sam spoke again.

"You call me if you see anything suspicious," he said with a frown, hand running over the top of his head to tug on his short pony tail. "Anything at all."

"Sure." Cici turned toward Justin. "Thanks for the lift."

Justin brought his eyes back down to Cici. "No prob. Let's get you home, Rev."

"Stick around and walk her dogs with her," Sam called out.

Justin threw a thumbs-up over his shoulder as he walked toward a police vehicle. He stayed right by her side as Cici opened her door and her hundred-plus-pound dogs tumbled out in a tangle of legs, tails, and doggy breaths.

True to his word, Justin stuck with Cici through her dog walk—which was much faster than usual because, much as it annoyed her, she worried about the exposure walking down the street garnered. She hated feeling so exposed…and unprepared.

The eerie feeling expanded as they turned the last corner back toward her house. Out front was a large, black pickup. It was wedged between Justin's police car and a compact sedan. Cici's steps slowed when Justin cursed, low and vicious.

"Do you know who that is?" she asked, trying to keep her voice level. Hard to do with the adrenaline dump that now pumped through her veins. She didn't need that spot in her head pinging *danger!* for Cici to realize the black beast of a truck growling mere feet from her doorstep meant trouble.

Justin shook his head as he half-stepped in front of her, causing the hairs on Cici's arms to rise. He might not know the person in the truck—hard to see through the dark tint—but the vehicle clearly upset him as much as her.

Mona backed up against Cici's leg while Rodolfo tugged at the end of his leash, his snarl deep and guttural.

The driver's side window rolled down about three inches. Cici squinted, but all she made out was a dark beanie pulled low over the person's eyebrows, and large, black plastic sunglasses.

The person threw something out the window. Rodolfo leaped forward, tugging the leash from Cici's hand as she flinched back. The dog sprinted toward the truck.

"Rodolfo, heel!" Cici called. The dog quivered to a halt, whining, as the truck's engine roared. Within seconds, it sped down the street.

Cici's breathing remained labored as she hurried forward, snatching up Rodolfo's leash. The dogs whined again and nuzzled against her, bumping her hips with their heads.

Justin snatched the paper from the street. He stood there, at the curb, scanning the message.

"Did you get the license plate?" Cici asked.

Justin shook his head, still staring after the truck. "Covered in mud or something." He swallowed, glanced down at the paper in his hand.

"What does that say?"

"I'm not sure you should read it."

"Not really your choice." Cici switched the dog leash to one hand and held out her free one. "The person came to *my* home. The message is clearly for me."

Justin handed it over with obvious reluctance.

Your sister didn't know when to stop snooping.

8

Listen to many, speak to a few. — Shakespeare

Justin called in the event once they entered Cici's house. While he was on the phone, she fed her dogs, before settling at her small kitchen table to pet their silky ears. Mona laid her head in Cici's lap, her large brown eyes boring into Cici's.

"Sam wants to come over now," Justin said, handing over the speaker.

Cici shook her head. "It can wait."

Justin frowned, opened his mouth. Sam must have said something into the phone because Justin pressed it closer to his ear.

"Say again? Okay. Yeah, that's smart. Uh uh. Uh huh. Yep. Bye."

Justin hung up, but the preoccupied expression settled more firmly on his face. Cici studied him for a moment before deciding to let him tell her whatever he and Sam discussed.

"Want to stay for pizza?" Cici asked.

"Sure."

Cici picked up the phone and ordered a large sausage and green chile pizza on whole wheat crust. When the meal arrived, they settled onto the couch to watch a movie. Justin tossed his crusts to the dogs, much to Cici's frustration—her dogs never received table scraps. Not because she didn't believe in sharing the wealth, but because she'd had to work hard to keep them from surfing her counters and dining table. But she bit her tongue because Justin was kind enough to stay.

She needed this level of kindness in her life right now.

After the movie credits rolled, Justin stood and stretched. He carried his glass and paper plate to the kitchen and set them on the counter.

"Time for me to go," he said.

Cici stared at him, wondering if there was a way for her to ask him to stay. If she did, it could change their relationship—one she hadn't considered since her sophomore year in high school when they dated briefly.

He'd wanted Anna Carmen more than her then, which had caused one of the biggest fights ever between the girls.

Before she managed to wrap her mind around whether she wanted Justin to stay, he said, "Someone from the department will be here to keep watch outside."

"All right. Hopefully I'll see you tomorrow at the early morning service," Cici said with a tremulous smile she didn't feel. "Blessings, Justin."

Justin leaned in and hesitated long enough for Cici to wonder if he meant to kiss her. He did, but on the cheek, as far from her lips as possible. Cici tried to stem the relief flowing through her body, not wanting it to flash into her eyes and upset him.

Justin shoved through the kitchen door and headed toward his car, not bothering to look back.

The next morning, Cici struggled to stay focused on her sermon—one of the worst, no *the* worst—she'd ever given. Her eyes kept flitting among the crowd, watching for nervous ticks, wondering who among them would want to scare her with dead birds and cruel notes.

When she finished, there was a collective sigh of relief. Her members hustled out of the sanctuary, many unwilling to meet her eyes as they headed toward their cars.

She rubbed her hand over her face, dreading facing the congregants.

"Not your best showing, Cee."

Sam's words brought her back to the present—standing in the atrium of her church as people laughed and shared coffee or a cookie around her.

"Why aren't you at mass?" she asked.

"Thought I'd check out the buzz around the hot new preacher in town. Gotta say, it seems overblown."

"Where's Jeannette?" Cici asked, craning her neck to find the sleek blonde.

"Since they have tomorrow off, she and a couple of her friends went up to Pagosa Springs. Be back late tomorrow."

Cici nodded.

"Want to grab some lunch?" Sam asked.

Cici sighed as she shook her head.

"Not today. But thanks."

From the corner of her eye, she saw Justin slip out the door. Sam followed her gaze, frowning.

"Everything okay there?"

"What? Oh, yeah. Fine."

"You sure, Cee? You look upset."

"Could have something to do with the mean note and dead birds."

She placed two fingers next to her temple, but the pressure didn't alleviate the pain that seemed to have taken up permanent residence there.

"I've got someone trailing you, staying at your place." Sam studied her. "I won't let anything happen to you, Cee."

On impulse, Cici leaned in, wrapping her arms around Sam's waist in a tight hug. Her head found his shoulder and his arms tightened, his cheek resting on her hair. She drew in the clean scent of his soap—she wasn't sure if it was body wash or detergent but it smelled fresh, woodsy. Safe.

The headache eased.

"I need to go talk to Evan," she choked out.

Sam stiffened. He stepped back, his hands remaining on her shoulders as he caught and held her gaze.

"Want me to come with you?" His voice was coaxing.

Cici almost caved. She did want him to, very much so. But… she doubted Evan would be as forthcoming in Sam's presence. Finally, she shook her head, regret stabbing her chest.

"No. I don't think you'll make this conversation with Evan any easier."

Sam dropped his arms and backed up farther. His expression turned inscrutable, much as it was any time she brought up Anna Carmen and Evan. Eventually, he shrugged.

"All right. I guess I'll see you soon. Stay safe."

Sam walked out the glass-paneled front doors, his hands shoved deep in his pockets.

———

Cici took a breath and smoothed down her nicest suit skirt—a lovely wool blend in neutral gray. Cici hated it, but it functioned as she needed it to. She looked respectable and about as professional as she could get.

She stepped into the law firm's foyer just after 8:00 a.m. She tried not to gawp at the opulence of the tumbled marble floors and pewter light fixtures. The chandelier hung with myriad bits of real crystal.

This place was grander than she'd expected—but it reminded her, with a sinking sensation, of her father's home with KaraLynn. She was the longest of her father's string of women who'd come during and after the divorce from Cici's mother.

This place, though, bustled with activity. Who knew lawyers were so busy early on a Monday morning?

Cici refused to go to her father's much more sedate law office here in Santa Fe once she realized her dad helped get potential criminals lighter sentences—or off completely. She'd been nine when she figured that out. She'd never been to his law office in Scottsdale, but she *hated* going to the residence her father had once shared with KaraLynn. She used to worry she'd spill on the white sofa or track dirt on the floor. After Anna Carmen's death, she couldn't stand that the last of her family proved so shallow and bothered by the inconsequentialities of life rather than celebrating uniqueness and what made each of them special.

"May I help you?" asked the receptionist, eyeing Cici's suit and trying, no doubt, to decide which lawyer Cici could possibly be here to see.

"Would you let Evan Reynolds know Reverend Cecilia Gurule is here. I don't have an appointment."

"Cici!"

James Roderick Pattison III called out her name, his eyes widening with delight.

"Dear me, I don't see you near often enough, my girl."

"Blessings, J.R. I missed speaking to you at Donald's funeral. How's your lovely wife? I spoke with Carina briefly after the service yesterday, so I know she and the baby are well."

"Joan said you visited our sweet pea with her sweet pea in the hospital and brought her a onesie and a blanket you knitted for the baby, too. You always were a thoughtful one, Cici. What brings you in?"

All this time, the receptionist's eyes widened more and more so now they took up most of her face. Guess it wasn't every day a stranger walked in and was greeted with such enthusiasm by the most successful partner in the firm.

"Well, I did want to be sure to invite Carina and Joan to our new mother/grandmother group. We have an amazing set of women."

"That's what Joan said. She's really pleased with the work you're doing at the church, Cici. That opening coming when it did—we're sure glad we were able to snap you up. I'm sure your mother would be just as proud as Joan is to have helped reel you back home."

Cici's smile widened. "That's high praise, J. R., and I'm

thrilled to hear it. I'm here to see Evan. If he's available."

"I'll make sure he is. Your time's just as valuable as his. Come on." He waved me past the still-gawking receptionist, who scrambled to look busy as we headed toward the bank of elevators across the lobby. J.R. leaned in, closer and said in a low voice, "Now, what's this I hear about Donald's death being like Anna Carmen's?"

Cici startled but turned toward him. Under his bushy white eyebrows were the keen eyes of a lifelong prosecutor. Sure, he handled mostly divorce and inheritance cases now—taking his lifestyle from comfortable to as lavish as many of his clients—but J.R. Pattison's name still brought the right kind of respect when he entered any courthouse in the state.

"You talked to Evan," Cici murmured. She paused, considering her options.

J.R.'s scowl turned blacker than the thunderheads that sat on Baldy throughout the summer.

"I did. After I saw him talking to you at Donald's funeral. I'm worried about you, my dear. This mess seems to be building again, and I don't like where it's headed."

Cici blinked, shocked by J.R.'s blunt assessment.

"Why do I get the sense there's more to that statement?" Cici asked.

J.R. rubbed his smooth chin, further enunciating the wrinkles surrounding his mouth.

"I don't know. Just…a gut sense." His normally twinkling pale blue eyes were flat and narrowed. "Evan and Don had a blowout after Anna Carmen's death."

Cici wondered if the bottom of the elevator dropped out...
no, just her legs turning to jelly.

"They did?"

J.R. patted her shoulder. "I almost had to let Evan go—
couldn't get rid of Don what with him being a partner and all.
But Don's the one who talked me out of it. Said Evan had a right
to be angry. Look, I don't have any details, but I'll investigate
Don's dealings. I have a feeling his work had something to do
with all this."

This conversation had not gone how Cici expected. "Why?"

"I promised your father if I heard anything—anything at all—
to bring that murdering rabble to justice; I'd do the legal leg work."

"My dad?" Cici squeaked.

J.R.'s face fell into heavy lines of grief. "I've never seen Frank
so low. Granted, Joan and I are still devastated by Anna Carmen's
death. Carina had nightmares for weeks."

They stepped out of the elevator.

Carina, J.R.'s only child and a good friend of both Anna
Carmen's and Cici's, was one of the people with Anna Carmen
on the pilgrimage to the Santuario. And one of the last people
to ever speak to her twin. Cici tried not to be jealous Carina had
those beautiful memories, but sometimes, like now, the pain of
losing Anna Carmen ate at her, making it hard not to be upset.

"And Cici." J.R. cleared his throat. "I'm worried. I mean,
Sam's back, as are you, which is wonderful—you're both great
people with good heads on your shoulders."

The weight of his stare crushed against Cici's chest.

"But, Anna Carmen's death wasn't an accident."

He paused, making sure Cici grasped the warning in those words.

"There's a reason Anna Carmen's killer wasn't found. Just as there's a reason Evan is still *here*, in this office, instead of taking that job he salivated for in Scottsdale."

Cici's mouth dried faster than water spilled on a summer-heated Albuquerque street. She studied his piercing eyes as he remained stoically silent.

She dipped her head. Message received. The shiver that built along Cici's spine swept through her chest cavity, biting cold and just as sinister.

———

"Cecilia," Evan said, rising from his desk, his nostrils flaring a little as he came around to take her hand in his larger one. He placed a kiss on her cheek, but Cici understood that show was for J.R., who'd tapped on Evan's office door.

J.R. nodded to Cici. "Joan and Carina will see you later this week, I'm sure."

With that, he lumbered down the hall as only a big and tall man can.

"To what do I owe the pleasure?" Evan asked, unbuttoning his suit jacket as he settled back into his plush leather chair. His hair was slicked down on his head, a shade or two darker than its natural color, thanks to the pomade. Cici wanted to reach over and dishevel it, simply to make Evan look more human—more caring. How had Anna Carmen been okay with Evan like this, with this lifestyle?

"Someone threw a note at me while I was walking my dogs."

Evan's mouth flattened. "God. What's the city coming to?"

Cici edged farther into the room. "I thought you should read it."

She laid the photocopy of the note on the desk. Evan picked it up slowly, his brows tightening over his nose as he read the words.

Cici sank into the leather-and-wood chair across from the large, ornate statement desk Evan reigned over. Her chair was lower, in case she needed a further reminder of who was in charge here.

"What did you mean?" she asked. "Your words Saturday, they bothered me. About Anna Carmen and Donald."

Evan steepled his index fingers in front of his mouth. He leaned forward, his eyes narrowed. "They spent time together in those last few days before her murder."

"Why?" Cici asked.

Evan shrugged, but his eyes cooled further, turned flinty. He knew something but wasn't willing to share. Fine. She knew that he knew more, and now he knew that she knew—as would the SFPD.

"Why didn't you take that position in Scottsdale? Weren't you set to go in two weeks?"

Evan stood, rebuttoning his coat. "My first morning appointment is here." He dipped his head toward the voices in the hallway. "If you want to catch up further, why don't you make an appointment with my secretary."

Cici stood, her heart hammering. "Fine. Anna Carmen told me about the engagement, you know."

Evan stopped, his shoulders stiffened.

"Your sister and I were *nothing* by the time she died. She made sure of that."

He stared down at her, this the face of the man who'd called her sister vile names.

"What happened to you, Evan?" Cici asked, her voice choked with emotion.

She assumed he wouldn't answer, so she began to walk toward the door.

As she passed him, he reached out and slammed his palm on the door jamb opposite her, caging her with his body.

"I got schooled in what betrayal means, Cee. You'd be smart to remember who taught *me* the lesson."

9

I am not bound to please thee with my answers.
— Shakespeare

Evan's words echoed in Cici's mind. Betrayal. Did he think Anna Carmen cheated on him?

With Donald Johnson? That made no sense.

While the twins had made a point to avoid each other's boyfriends, that didn't mean they hadn't found the same men attractive. Justin had been the only exemption. He'd liked Anna Carmen better—dumped Cici for her twin—which caused Cici not to speak to Anna Carmen for the entire month the two dated.

But Anna Carmen had talked to Cici before she'd accepted that first date. Cici had been sad, but more embarrassed by getting dumped by the boy *she* liked. Back then, Cici's name meant trouble. That was part of the reason she hadn't attended college in her home town to stay and support her dying mother. Cici had wanted adventure—maybe some wildness—while Anna Carmen had craved an organized sock drawer.

Cici remained too worked up from her conversation with Evan to go home. After visiting two of her church members who were in the hospital—one for a hip replacement, the other receiving chemotherapy—Cici decided to lunch with Mrs.

Hodgkins at one of the retirement communities in town. The woman complained about the waitress's service, the blandness of the food, and even the ugliness of the new carpet, but Cici didn't mind. The woman just wanted someone to listen to her—to agree that her opinions and autonomy mattered.

The clock slipped past one when Cici arrived home and changed into a T-shirt, jeans, and low-heeled boots. She took Mona and Rodolfo for a short walk, but the dogs tugged on their leashes, tongues hanging far out of their mouths as the animals sought shade or, better yet, the cool Saltillo tile of her living room.

Cici added ice to their water bowls and left them happily crunching away, knowing they loved the cool cubes. She tugged on her leather gloves and jacket before pulling her Harley out of the garage. She buckled her helmet and then headed up 284 before turning onto 504 and making a quick stop at the falls in Nambé. After watching the cold mountain water pour down on laughing children and adults in the afternoon sunshine, Cici climbed back on her motorcycle and headed northeast toward Chimayó.

Her phone beeped in the pocket of her jeans. Sam, no doubt, asking why she'd left the city limits and the jurisdiction of her police escort.

She ignored the phone, focusing instead on the feeling in her chest, the awareness in her mind. Anna Carmen seemed closer than usual. As if…as if she was guiding Cici to something monumental.

Cici passed the sign that told of the Pueblo tribes that settled the area hundreds, possibly thousands of years before the second arrival of Spanish descendants. The area's long weaving history was noted as well. Years ago, Cici's mother brought her and Anna Carmen to the area to watch masters work in various textiles. The thoughts, like many Cici carried, made her sad.

Red chile pepper *ristras* hung from the local store and from the thick vigas holding up the front porch of a local bed-and-breakfast.

Cici pulled into the lot of the large Santuario. With a steadying breath, she removed her helmet, set in on the seat of her motorcycle, and headed toward the front doors.

After walking through the adobe arch and into the main sanctuary, Cici crossed herself, as was her family's custom whenever they visited the church. She sat in a pew in the middle of the sanctuary, letting the silence clarify her thoughts. She stared at the image of Jesus nailed to the cross and shuddered. From there, she looked at the brightly painted wooden scenes surrounding the depicted death of the Savior.

Unfortunately, her thoughts bounded around even faster than her eyes could peruse the large wooden wall of images. Evan's words continued to orbit through Cici's head.

She was missing something—*something* that caused Evan to turn bitter and cold. Something that made J.R. want to protect Cici.

Cici sat up straighter. Something the law firm knew or *possibly* knew about Anna Carmen's death…or what led to it…

No. Something about Donald Johnson.

Out of the corner of her eye, she caught a slight shifting of movement. When she turned to look, no one was there. Frowning, Cici faced forward again, and the outline of a woman…of her sister, sharpened in the dim space.

"What did Donald know?" Cici murmured aloud. "Is that what got you killed? Did you give him information or did he give it to you?"

Cici didn't know. And Anna Carmen wasn't telling. Nope, she didn't even try to speak to Cici this time.

"Susan Johnson doesn't seem to know," Cici huffed out. "But that didn't mean someone in the community was ignorant of Donald's actions—and the part he played in Anna Carmen's death."

A cool, soft draft slid over Cici's hand. Like…almost like Anna Carmen was trying to clasp it.

Cici breathed in and out in slow, measured puffs, needing to control her breathing and calm her racing thoughts enough to stand, to exit this place.

"I need you to guide me," Cici said. "I wish you'd told me more last year." Her eyes filled with tears, but Cici blinked them back until she could see the altar clearly once more. "I wish you'd trusted me with whatever problem you had. I miss you, Aci."

Cici walked from the centuries-old church feeling more drained than when she entered. She texted Sam as concisely as possible her revelations of the day.

Where are you? he asked.

In Chimayó. Be home in a couple of hours.

Be careful, he replied and she could practically hear the censure through those words. *And let me know when you get home.*

Instead of turning toward her motorcycle, she walked back down the road. A dangerous decision because the sun began to lower in the sky. With some guess work and guidance from that strange, cool air, she found the approximate spot where her twin had died, trying to channel more of Anna Carmen's emotions.

Nothing came.

"I don't understand what's going on," Cici murmured, willing her sister to answer. "Just that it's bad and it's still happening."

If Anna Carmen remained nearby—if *el Señor* was listening— no one planned to answer Cici's questions today. After the third car whizzed past, honking in a long peel of angry motorist horn, Cici gave up. She also realized just how hungry she was.

She stopped at Gabriel's on the way home for some of their guacamole, which the waiter made table side. She ate it and her chicken and rice slowly, more picking at her food. Much as she longed for a cold local brew—maybe a Santa Fe Pen Porter— she'd never drink an alcoholic beverage while on her sister's motorcycle.

She smiled down into her iced tea, thinking that was one of the best lessons her father taught her. At least, one of the few positive ones that stuck.

After zipping up her leather jacket and slipping back on her gloves, Cici rode home at a sedate pace, trying to wrap her head around Anna Carmen's presence—then immediate disappearance. As she stopped at the deserted intersection of Paseo de Peralta and St. Francis, that cool brush of wind intermixed with the much warmer summer air. Cici glanced around, wondering where the chill originated because it felt just like the cold touch on her hand in the Santuario.

A truck—the same dark tinted windows, dark exterior that

had appeared at her house the evening she walked with Justin and her dogs—sped up as it entered the intersection from her left. The large engine revved loud as a roar as the back wheels squealed. The headlights aimed at Cici. A car kitty-corner to the black truck—the one with the green light, laid on his horn, alerting the rest of the cars now heading this direction to slow.

Good. At least innocent people wouldn't be hurt.

Cici guessed it would be just five seconds until impact, maybe less. Probably, she wouldn't be able to avoid impact, but no way she planned to wait there another moment and simply let someone flatten her.

She grasped the handlebars and squeezed the gas as hard as she could. Turbo injection—a nonstandard addition Anna Carmen made a few years ago to add some more zip to the machine—kicked in and Cici blasted sideways, up onto the sidewalk and into the field behind Gonzales Community School.

Cici screamed as her bike jumped the curb, then hit the rock-strewn field with a teeth-rattling thud. She squinted, trying to keep her eyes focused on the space in front of her after the truck's front chrome fender missed her by mere inches. Her heart revved near as fast as the engine of her Harley as she wove around the chain link fence surrounding the school.

The truck tore over the rough terrain, spitting bits of gravel and broken sticks in all directions. Some hit Cici's helmet, making a horrendous pinging sound.

Cici squeezed the throttle harder and the engine shrilled as she took as hard a turn on the bike as she dared. She couldn't outrun that big truck engine. Her tires skittered and Cici worked to regain better control of the bike.

The truck revved, sounding closer.

Cici gulped. Few choices. None good.

She'd been here, at this school, last week to read to the kids. The teacher—a friend of hers and Anna Carmen's—had pointed out a gap in the chain-link that led onto the playground.

Where was it? Far to the back, used to let older kids into the playground for the activities they didn't want their parents or the school lights to discover.

The truck roared behind her, close enough for Cici to feel the heat through her leather jacket.

There. She nearly missed the gap. Holding her breath, Cici veered her motorcycle through it, shrinking her body as tight against the motorcycle. The leather on her gloves and jacket ripped before the points of the chain-link managed to gouge the skin from the back of her hands and her forearms, but Cici bit hard on her lip as she shot through the wire and into the relative safety of the field.

Until the truck plowed through the fence.

As she wove around the tetherball posts, she screamed as loudly as she could, "Anna Carmen, I am really mad at you!"

Cici cut around the school, nearly hitting the corner of the building and its protruding brown bricks as she jumped another curb onto the sidewalk and then slammed back into the parking lot. Much as she wanted to look behind her, she focused on veering around the center median.

With a quick prayer to the God who seemed to have neglected her these last few heart-thumping minutes, she flew onto West Alameda, cringing as heat from exhaust and moving cars bombarded her. More honking horns, this time followed by angry, raised voices cursing her as she sped along the bike lane and then jumped another curb onto the river trail and into the Alto Youth Center. Finally, she slowed the motorcycle to a more sedate forty miles per hour.

Sirens blared from somewhere behind her. Cici drew a deep breath. Her palms were slicked with sweat and blood. Her fingers, stiff and white, remained wrapped around the black plastic of the handle grips.

Home.

She just wanted to get home. To her dogs and the relative safety of her small house.

Her breath came in short pants, and as she turned onto Urioste Street, heading toward Agua Fria, she finally got up the gumption to look in her small side mirror.

The black truck, the demon beast that would haunt her nightmares for months yet to come, was nowhere to be seen.

10

No legacy is so rich as honesty. — *Shakespeare*

Cici called Sam as soon as she pulled her Harley into the garage.

"You did *what*?"

Cici locked her knees, unable yet to climb off the motorcycle. Her heart beat faster than any Maria Benitez flamenco routine—and twice as hard.

"Like I had a choice, Samuel. That truck came at me—even plowed through the fence. It wanted to plow through *me*." The last word ended in somewhere between a shout and a wail.

Holy See and all the saints…Cici could not believe she was alive and in one piece. She frowned at the bloody coverings over her hands and arms. Mostly in one piece.

Better than she'd expected when that cold breeze hit her neck.

Cici gulped, so thankful for this chance to breathe, to think. To be mad at Sam.

"I just heard about this," Sam said on a sigh. "Christ—"

"Watch it!"

Cici managed to totter off her bike and move into her kitchen. She planted her butt in the closest chair as Sam spoke into her ear, his voice dripping with annoyance—and…could it be? He sounded…scared.

"You say worse than that," Sam said. "Stay put. I'll need to get a full statement. And, for God's sake, stop getting into trouble, will you?"

"Like I ask for it," Cici muttered, hanging up the phone.

She'd had her fill of Sam-talk for the night.

The doorbell rang.

Cici froze.

She fumbled with her phone, ready to redial Sam's number.

What if the person in the black truck was out there—on her small porch—now?

She crept forward, her finger hovering over the "Talk" icon.

Silencing her dogs, Cici walked through her living room to peek out the small window. Relief swamped her, making her limbs heavy. Tears burned up her nose. An adrenaline crash, Cici decided. She huffed as she slid her phone into her pocket. Then, she opened the front door.

"Can we talk, Rev?" Juan Sanchez stood on her small wooden porch, hands tucked into his frayed jeans pockets.

"Sure." Cici stepped aside to let the hulking teen into her home. "What's this about?"

He swallowed hard, a heavy sound full of emotion that eclipsed the ticking of the dogs' feet on the tile floors as they settled into comfortable positions.

"It's about your sister."

Juan fidgeted before Rodolfo shoved his leonine head against Juan's thigh, nuzzling closer both to offset Juan's nervousness but also because the big, white dog liked to be pet. All day, every day. The teenager scratched Rodolfo's head and the dog's eyes narrowed in bliss and his tongue flopped from his mouth as he smiled.

"You weren't here then—when it happened. But you know Marco died of an opioid overdose. They said…the police said he downed a whole bottle of Demerol in the boys' bathroom at the start of football practice. By the time anyone found him, he was…"

Juan swallowed and wiped his eyes with his thumb.

"My dad yanked me from Capitol that next week. Sent me to Saint Michael's. He didn't want me mixed up in Marco's mess."

Cici nodded as she settled into her brown leather club chair opposite the loveseat where the teen settled his size forty bulk. Mona pressed against Cici's side, not liking the attention her brother was receiving. Cici pet the dog's soft, feathery ears.

A moment later, Mona turned and began to lick Cici's hands and forearms, laving away the sweat and dried blood. Cici wished she kept whiskey in the house—she could really use a shot of something bracing right now.

But she didn't do hard liquor.

"So young," she murmured, hating the idea of this young man going through the same grief process Cici struggled to overcome each day. "I'm so sorry for your loss, Juan. I know how hard it is to lose a sibling. And I know how lame my words sound…how uninspired and not enough."

"I…I miss him."

Cici leaned forward. "Of course, you do."

Juan cleared his throat. "Not why I'm here. We were cleaning out the old trailer. Me and my dad." Add in Mrs. Sanchez, and that equated to the young man's entire family. Not unlike Cici's own shrunken relative pool.

"All right. That's good."

Juan shrugged. "Maybe. Dad says we gotta move out of Abuelita's neighborhood. He can't stand all the rich bit…er, older people." Juan's face flushed as did his neck. "Er, sorry, Rev."

"I've thought some of those Acequia Madre folks were bitchy myself a time or two."

Juan startled and Cici bit back a smile. "Oh. Right. You grew up over there. Dad don't like it. So, we went back to our property out on Brickman. Where we still got the old trailer and stuff. Anyway, Dad says we gotta clean it so we can live in it again."

Mona stood and walked around to Cici's other side where she once again began bathing Cici's broken skin. Juan's gaze followed this time and his eyes widened.

"What happened to you?" he gasped.

"Met a fence that didn't like me. My bike's scratched up."

Cici frowned. That was the first time she'd thought of the Harley as hers. Did it matter? She wasn't sure, but owning it, caring for it, riding it to its limit seemed crucial somehow. Like… well, like the motorcycle wanted to be hers.

Or maybe that Anna Carmen wanted it to be Cici's.

Cici bit her lip as she watched Mona's pink tongue lave her broken skin. Yes, Anna Carmen passed the bike to her tonight. Officially.

Cici had to blink back tears. Now wasn't the time for her own baggage.

What had she and Juan been talking about? Right. The move

back to the family's trailer off Brickman.

"Are you happy about that move, Juan? I know they can be hard."

The teen shrugged. "Don't care so much where my bed is, Rev. I mean, I liked Abuelita's fine. It's closer to Jaycee, her being down near Madrid."

He flushed a little. Jaycee and Juan had begun dating toward the end of the past school year. He was such a big guy—rarely spoke unless he needed to—and Jaycee was bubbly, an effervescent force. They made an adorable high school couple. Only time would tell if they could manage the eighty-mile separation when Jaycee started at UNM and Juan at Tech in another year—at least those were the top schools of choice the teenagers mentioned last time Cici had asked. And they'd need to make it through their senior year first, but Juan and Jaycee seemed solid. Now.

Cici frowned, remembering the hurt in Evan's eyes before he shut down on Cici this morning.

What had her sister been involved in?

Why hadn't Anna Carmen told Cici about her concerns?

Juan yanked some faded, ripped papers from his back pocket and shoved them into Cici's hands. Cici had to bite her tongue to keep from yelping. Paying attention—being present as she always preached—proved impossible for her to do tonight.

"Anyways, when we were cleaning stuff today…," Juan said. "We wouldn't have ever found 'em except Dad dropped his end of the bed when we hauled it out of the trailer."

Juan shifted his eyes around the room, his lips twitching.

"Dad said it's divine intervention, him deciding this now, and then us finding these. He said you needed to know."

"Divine intervention," Cici murmured, thinking of her sister and the brushes of cold air earlier tonight. "You said you found these in the late afternoon?"

"Yeah."

When she was sitting in the chapel in Chimayó begging her sister to give her something. She shook her head as she shuffled through the papers. *Not quite what I had in mind, Aci.*

If her sister had a hand in whatever Juan gave Cici at all. Either way, that's what Cici deserved for not being more specific about what she wanted from her sister.

Two newspaper clippings, a PO Box number, and hand-written notes. Anna Carmen's *essence*—for lack of a better word—jumped out of the scrawl, causing Cici's neck to tingle.

"Where were these?" Cici asked around her clogged throat.

"Shoved in a hole in Marco's mattress. He wasn't secretive, Rev. Least I didn't think he was." Juan swallowed, his Adam's apple bobbing with the effort.

"Your sister was helping out my brother, see. Dad said to bring it to you. He doesn't want any of that drug sh…er, stuff tainting me. I'm looking to get a full ride to Tech. I really want to work for NASA."

Cici set the papers onto the small coffee table with trembling hands. Juan slammed a key down on top of it, causing Cici to jump and Mona to yip. Both dogs stood, tails up and eyes wary.

"I think that's the key to the post office box. Marco told me he had to go back, check it for Miss Gurule."

Juan hung his head, tears dripping off the end of his nose.

Anger built in his words—probably in the reason he slammed down the key—but so did grief. The poor child. Cici reached forward and clutched the teen's hands, which were as cold and shaky as her own.

"I don't know if he ever did," Juan whispered. "Mom went out that night, and…well, you've heard that story."

"Do you know which post office?" Cici asked.

Juan shook his head.

Cici clutched Juan's hands tighter. She did know that story. Rosalia Sanchez's body turned up in the trickle of water Santa Feans insisted on calling a river, up near the large park on East Alameda. A jogger found her the next morning, her throat slit, but no one uncovered a motive.

"He was my idol, Rev," Juan said, his voice thick. "Miss Gurule's the one who got him in advance classes and in the medical program over there at Capitol."

The young man rubbed his eyes. "He shoulda graduated last year."

"Yes, he should have." And Cici should be able to hug her sister. Life wasn't fair.

"Marco adored Miss Gurule. You gotta find out what they were working on. 'Cause it got 'em both killed."

11

I say there is no darkness but ignorance.
— Shakespeare

Sam had stopped by moments later, while Juan Sanchez was still in her living room. She opened the door but blocked the entrance.

"Talk later?" Cici asked. "I have something here I need to handle."

Sam eyed Juan with concern over Cici's shoulder before his gaze refocused on Cici's.

"All right. We have an APB out on the truck. Not that it seems to be doing us much good."

"Thanks, Sam," Cici said, her voice subdued. "I'll call you."

He nodded to both Cici and Juan, who watched their interaction with wary eyes.

"You better," Sam said. "Tonight."

Cici nodded as she leaned against the door. Sam slid his thumb down her cheek in silent comfort before jogging down her front steps.

She closed the door with slow, careful movements, trying to recalibrate her world. Juan's story bothered her. Then, now. Always. Had she been so caught up in her own grief that she missed the needs of this teenager?

She and Juan talked for a while longer. Well, he did most of the talking while Cici tried to be a good listener. But her mind kept drifting back to the notes in what she was sure was Anna Carmen's handwriting, to the black truck and the note tossed so casually from the cab.

She called Sam. He declined coming over but he did make her go through the entire timeline twice, from the drive up to Chimayó to her return home. Once he was satisfied she could offer no further information, Cici's mouth was dry and her eyelids felt weighted down with lead.

She picked up the papers Juan tossed on the coffee table. She sifted through them, her eyes roving, noting…not understanding.

She blew out a breath and let her tired eyes slide shut.

Maybe the realization that her sister's fiancé believed she'd cheated with an older married man wasn't such bad news after all. Not when the alternative was her sister involving a young boy in a dangerous drug ring. But there was no doubt that the first page of papers Juan sent was a list in Anna Carmen's handwriting. Cici opened her eyes, looking at the list again.

2-PS

5-SFPM

3-DVM

3-NRD

2-IPR

3-MS

Another page offered maps of Santa Fe, Española, and Madrid. Tiny red dots overlaid the maps, making the street names below hard to read.

Cici set all three of the maps out on her table, shuffling them, trying to make sense of the papers.

Nothing.

She picked up the news clippings that outline details of her twin receiving the Santa Fe Public School's Teacher of the Year award. Cici ran her fingertips over the page, trying to ignore the trembling that set in.

Lights flashed through her front window and Cici grabbed all the materials Juan had given her, clutching them to her heaving chest before she realized it was just her neighbor pulling into his driveway.

Her dogs cocked their heads at her.

"Yeah, yeah. I'm a nut."

Cici carefully folded each of the papers and walked down her short hallway. She shoved them into the pillowcase of the pillow that laid on the unused left-hand side of her queen bed. After ensuring that each of her doors was locked—and the windows, too—she trudged back to her bathroom where she took a quick shower, wincing as the hot water hit the cuts and abrasions on her hands and arms. Once dry and bandaged, Cici fell into her bed.

Her furniture used to be Anna Carmen's. Cici had sold her teak bedroom set back in Boston, hoping this older, white wicker set of her sister's would bring the woman closer to her—at least in slumber.

And Cici did dream of her sister—often.

She did so again, that night.

Cici dreamed she was one of those white birds. Whole

and pretty, soaring through the large open blue expanse of the Northern New Mexican sky.

Anna Carmen veered in closer. She opened her bird beak wide, and the words seemed to pour from her.

"Here, you are the white bird. That means you'll find your soulmate. The question is: Are you courageous enough to go and get him? I had mine."

Somehow, her black bird eyes morphed into Anna Carmen's hazel ones, filled with sorrow.

"But I wasn't ready to accept all that came with Evan."

Cici frowned. Courageous enough? It wasn't a question she wanted to think about right now. She wanted to hear as much of her sister's voice as possible, to feel safe as she always had in Anna Carmen's presence.

"What do you mean? What do you mean you weren't brave enough?" Cici asked.

"I wanted more than I should have," Anna Carmen replied, her voice melancholy. "I wanted to protect my students, their families, but in the process, I lost sight of what was truly important. Do you know what that is?"

Anna Carmen's beautiful hazel eyes stared out of the bird's sharp features. There was a strange pop. Anna Carmen fell, her eyes never leaving Cici's face. Cici screamed as she dived toward her sister, only then realizing the sound was gun shots—many of them—in rapid succession.

"Don't follow me. You can't save me. I didn't understand the danger. Don't follow!"

But it was too late. The pain burst in Cici's chest, causing her breath to shatter and her wings falter. She couldn't spread her wings. She couldn't breathe. Her sister's eyes disappeared into the black as Cici fell.

And she was in her bed, gasping for breath.

Her dogs stood at the window, hackles raised and teeth bared so that the sharp points of their canines flashed in the dark.

Cici rose with care. She tottered toward the window.

A form rose to fill the space. Darkness swirled around the figure, save the whites of its eyes, which shone even brighter than the dogs' fangs.

The person in black raised something in a gloved hand. Something that glinted in the moonlight. A knife—like the one that had killed Anna Carmen. Its blade was about three inches long, silver, the moonlight slithering off each side of the sharp edge.

A single word was smeared in red—*please don't let it be blood*—on the glass: Stop.

Cici staggered back, screaming. Rodolfo leaped onto the sill and barked. Cici put her hands to her ears to block out the dog's supersonic boom.

A light flared, followed by voices yelling, "Get down! Police!"

But the figure seemed to melt back into the shadows, leaving Cici standing there, at her window, shivering in her perspiration-soaked pajamas.

———

Sam called Cici a few minutes later. Cici managed to answer the call but put him on speaker because her hands weren't steady enough to hold the phone to her ear.

"Good God, woman, there's been quite a procession you had

at your place tonight."

Cici started. Then warmth broke through the iciness attacking her chest and gut.

"You've been here this whole time?" she asked.

"Like there's any other place I'd rather stake out."

"Why?" Cici whispered.

"Because someone tried to run you over," Sam said.

Cici touched her hair before she trailed her trembling fingers across her cheek. "You should have told me. I'd have invited you in."

"Defeats the purpose of a stakeout, Cee. I wanted to see the comings and goings."

Her heart warmed further as she heard the smile in his voice. Oh, she'd needed that—something positive to latch on to. "Did you…did you get the person?"

Cici heard Sam's long and loud sigh through the phone. "No. But I wasn't the one chasing the perp. That's all on Officer Loomis."

"Don't be mad at Kevin, Sam. He's barely twenty-one."

"And he lost me the best lead on this case," Sam bit back.

"Will you come in now?" Cici asked, her voice trembling. "I…" She sucked in a deep breath, held it until her tummy quivered. "I'm so scared," she choked out.

"Yeah." So much emotion in that word—emotion Cici didn't know how to unpack and pick apart. But that was okay. Sam was coming. "Everyone would expect you to call me," he continued, "so there's no point in me sitting in this cold car. Will you get me a blanket and a pillow?"

Cici smiled at the phone where it lay on her bed. Some of the fear lifted and a swell built in her chest, spreading warmth. "A step ahead of you, hombre."

"I'm at the door. Let me in."

Cici scooped up her phone and headed toward the front door, the shaking in her limbs easing with each step.

Rodolfo stood nearby, wagging his long, plume-y tail. When Sam stepped into the house, Rodolfo whined in joy, shoving his large head against Sam's thigh. Mona refused to be left out and pushed forward to nudge Sam for attention. He petted them both while Cici maneuvered behind him to shut and lock the front door.

She opened her mouth to offer to make him tea, but Sam looked dead on his feet. After a glance at the clock, Cici winced in sympathy. Two in the morning was not the best time for long chats or deep discussions. She spread the blankets on the couch. Sam lay down before she shoved the pillow into its case.

His breathing evened out after she arranged his head on the pillow.

"How long have you been watching my place?" she asked.

"All week," he mumbled, snuggling into the pillow. "Since we found Donald."

———

"What did Juan want last night?" Sam asked as he waltzed into her kitchen the next morning. His hair stuck out all over his head and his eyelids were puffy from lack of sleep. The rumpled clothes and pillow creases on his cheek added to his overall dishevelment. He didn't look like a successful police detective—at the moment, he was about half a step up from people locking their car doors or pedestrians crossing the street in reaction to seeing him.

Still, Cici remained glad for his presence.

She slid her hand into her jeans pocket and squeezed the key in her fist. "About that."

Her stomach howled louder than a coyote with a cut paw.

Sam chuckled. "All right. Breakfast first and then we can discuss whatever Juan told you."

"It's almost lunch time."

Sam startled. "Ten-thirty-three? Why didn't you wake me?"

"Because you said you've been sitting outside my house all week. Seemed like you deserved some uninterrupted shut-eye."

"Thanks. I'll buy you lunch for your hospitality. I hope I didn't mess up your day."

"Nah. I've been slow to get moving. I didn't sleep much. I kept thinking about Anna Carmen," Cici murmured. "She's in my every thought."

Sam stayed quiet for a long moment.

"I dreamed of her last night. She was a white bird, shot out of the sky," he said.

Cici faced him. "I dreamed that, too. I was there. A bird."

"My job was to stop the hunter," Sam said, shoving his hands deep into his pockets. "I didn't get to him fast enough to save Anna Carmen."

"Sam—"

He shook his head. "Talking to the dead." He hauled in a deep breath. "That's voo-doo witchery, and I don't like it. But, yeah… Anna Carmen's trying to make sure I know this is important—that you need protection."

He cleared his throat because his voice had thickened. His gaze, when it met hers, was serious, determined.

"I should have listened to you after Donald's funeral. I'm sorry I didn't. But I won't let you down, Cee. I promise."

"We have to find out who killed Anna Carmen," Cici said, blinking back her tears. "That's the key to this. Whoever killed her is involved in Donald's death. I know it."

Instead of arguing with her, Sam nodded. "Let's talk it over at lunch."

———

Twenty minutes later, after Sam showered and Cici finished getting herself ready, Cici locked up the house, the dogs happy to wait inside in the relative coolness. She followed Sam to his small hybrid SUV. He opened the passenger door for her, and she slid into the tan leather interior. Sam remained one of the only males in her life to open doors. She wasn't sure if it was gentlemanly or just old-fashioned. Either way, she appreciated the gesture— probably because it was so rare.

Sam drove toward the Plaza. He pulled in to a side street and hopped out. Cici followed suit, slamming the SUV's door shut before she met him on the sidewalk.

"The Shed?" she asked, her voice hopeful.

"You bet. It's your favorite. And after last night, I figured you deserved it."

They waited for a table, neither talking much as Sam watched some football game on a big screen TV and Cici watched a family interact with their two small daughters.

"Twins?" she asked just as Sam's name was called by the hostess.

The mom glanced up, surprised. "How'd you know? They don't look anything alike."

"The way they interact. I'm…I was a twin."

The mom swallowed hard and hugged her daughters closer. Yeah, probably not the best ice breaker when meeting new people. Cici let Sam tug her to a small wooden table near the back of the restaurant. He ordered chips, salsa, guacamole, and two iced teas before Cici managed to slide her rear into the chair.

"Look over the menu and then order the posole like you always do. But hurry it up because I want to hear about whatever's preoccupied you to the point you haven't even asked about the perp last night."

Cici chose to fold her hands on top of the menu without picking it up. "Juan gave me some notes they found in an old mattress. He also gave me a PO Box key."

Sam leaned back in his chair, blue eyes narrowed. "That just turned up last night? After all this time? Marco died—"

"A few weeks before Anna Carmen."

The waiter dropped off their appetizer and drinks. Sam motioned to Cici and she asked for the chicken fajitas. Sam's eyebrows rose as he ordered the posole. Once the waiter wandered off to another of his tables, Sam said, "You really think this just came up?"

"I don't know." Cici swallowed hard. "Part of me thinks that crazy. But…Juan lost his mother and brother in a one-month span. I know his father moved them both in with Mrs. Sanchez in the little guest house behind the family's main residence on Cerro Gordo. So…yeah, it's possible they just got around to clearing out the trailer Miguel lived in with Rosalia, Marco, and Juan."

"Seems too convenient," Sam said on a scowl. He dunked a tortilla chip into the salsa and crunched through it.

"Didn't say it wasn't convenient, Sam-o. And I really wish you'd be more open to the option that Anna Carmen's helping. Not everything in life has nefarious underpinnings."

Cici picked up a chip of her own and broke off a small piece, dipping it into the creamy green guacamole. The flavors sung over her tongue as she chewed. Seriously best food in town.

"I have been open to Anna Carmen helping. I told you that back at your place."

Cici simply bit into her tortilla chip.

"Fine. I think it's weird, but I guess it's as likely for you—being identical—as those psychics."

Cici sat back in her chair and glared at Sam. "I'm no psychic."

"I know, which is why I tend to believe that Anna Carmen is trying—poorly, I might add—to help us from beyond the grave. The least she could do is use that twin-speak you two used to have down."

Cici licked her lips, her face taut.

"It's not like that," she whispered. "That level of connection severed when she died."

Cici's lip trembled, so she picked up her iced tea and took a long swallow.

"Cee, I didn't mean to upset you."

Sam reached for her hand. Cici let him grasp her fingers

because they were cold and she was tired of feeling so alone.

"But…there's something. It's…I don't think she ever left. Not completely. But, she's muted."

Sam leaned back, letting go of her hand. "Muted?"

Cici nodded. "She's doing what she can, Sam. Through dreams. Through…this sounds crazy. But she's the reason I maneuvered away from the truck last night. I…I felt her."

Sam's gaze searched her face, held her eyes for a long, painful moment. He dipped his head.

"All right."

Cici sagged back in her chair, relieved for his acceptance.

"You have a key and notes, you said. Can I seem 'em?" Sam's voice turned brusque. He didn't like the idea of communicating with the dead.

Cici pulled them from her jeans pocket and handed them over. Sam studied each note carefully. He flipped over the ripped pieces of paper to check the backs. He spread them out on the table and took pictures of them on his phone. "I'm assuming you did the same?" he said, motioning to the lens on his phone

"Of course. I saved the images to my computer and then sent another copy to my church email account."

"Covering your bases," Sam said with approval.

Cici saluted. "I've learned from the best."

Sam tilted the pages in different directions, studying details Cici didn't even begin to know about.

"I want to take these to the station," he said. "Get them looked over."

Cici nodded as she finished her chip and picked up her glass of tea.

Sam swiped the key off the table and studied it. A number, barely legible, shone against an old piece of peeling Scotch tape.

"We'll head on over after we eat."

"Head where?"

Sam tapped the key on the table. "The one on Pacheco first. It's the largest post office in town."

"But the one at DeVargas would have been closer to the Sanchez's trailer."

Sam pursed his lips. "We think someone's using the Pacheco Street post office to dump drugs."

"We do?"

Sam scowled. "Yes. The SFPD does. Now *we* do."

Cici crossed her arms. "Fine. How long do you think this person's been using the post office?"

Sam's gaze slid from hers back to the table, a frown building between his brows. Cici closed her eyes and shook her head.

"Oh. Really, Sam? Since Santa Fe Art and Design. What's that? More than a year?"

"That's my best guess," Sam said, his mouth turned down as he stared at the key.

"And no leads?" Cici asked.

Sam held up the key and then the papers. "You just handed two to me. I called in a search warrant request to one of the judges on-call."

"When?" Cici asked. Yes, she was aware Sam hadn't answered her question—but he had, in a way, when he'd brought up the opioid ring in Madrid earlier this week.

Sam appeared amused. "While you were telling that big oaf of a dog 'goodbye'."

The waiter dropped the fajitas at their table and Cici eyed Sam's posole hungrily. He passed her the dish without comment as he began filling one of the thick flour tortillas—his favorite.

"You're welcome," Cici said just before she shoved the spoonful of sinfully-spiced corn and pork into her mouth.

Sam chewed his bite and wiped his lips with a napkin. "So are you. And just for the record, Jeannette thinks I like chimi-changas."

"You two talk about her relationship with Donald?" Cici asked, her voice hesitant.

Sam took another bite of his fajita. He glanced up and shook his head. An intentional decision not to answer her question verbally. Fine, he didn't want to talk about his relationship with Jeannette. Fair enough.

"Why does she think anyone likes chimichangas?" Cici asked, wrinkling her nose. Those things were gross.

"No idea. But I can't tell you how many of those nasty things I've put away over the past year."

Laughing with a friend never felt so good.

After lunch—where Cici scraped out every bit of deliciousness from the posole bowl and Sam groaned his way through all the fajitas—they settled back in the car and headed back down St. Francis toward St. Michaels. A quick right turn led them onto one of the main thoroughfares through the heart of the city and

Sam moved into the left lane to turn onto Pacheco.

The post office was a block up on the left. For some reason, Cici tensed as they made the turn onto Pacheco.

That cool touch. This time to her cheek closest to the window. Cici shivered, glanced over and caught the glimpse of a large, black truck in the side mirror.

"Don't pull in," Cici said, gripping Sam's wrist hard enough for him to grunt.

"What the hell's gotten into you, Cici."

"Just drive down toward Siringo," she snapped, her hand wound tight on the door handle. That little brush on her cheek seemed stronger. The black truck was definitely closer.

Sam scowled but did as she asked. he made the right turn onto Siringo.

"Cut back to the church there." Cici pointed, not because she'd planned to or even wanted to—because her mind just knew that was the best course of action. *Aci?* Cici asked.

No answer.

Cici wanted to growl in frustration. But she refrained, mainly because the black truck closed the gap between the vehicles. Cici clutched the door handle, bracing for imminent impact.

"Why are we doing this?" Sam grumbled.

"A feeling."

"A *feeling?*" he snapped.

But Sam drove toward that parking lot. As he turned in, a large black truck with illegally dark windows shot past them so close, Sam and Cici jerked forward when the vehicle clipped Sam's SUV's bumper.

Cici yelped while Sam cursed. The loud rumble of the truck died as it sped back toward St. Francis Drive.

Sam unclenched his hands from the steering wheel. "Close call there."

"A warning," Cici said. "Same truck we saw in front of my house the other night. The one that tried to mow me down off my Harley."

Sam pulled into a spot and pushed the gearshift into park. "You get the license plate?"

Cici shook her head as she clasped her shaking hands in her lap. "Wasn't one on the front bumper."

"You sure it was the same truck?"

"Yes," Cici said.

"Well, now we know it's a Dodge Ram."

"You sure?" Cici asked.

"Yeah. That'll narrow down the search. But why's the driver getting bolder?"

Sam pursed his lips but apparently chose not to question her further. Instead, much to Cici's unease, he reached over her legs to unlock his glove compartment. From there, he drew his police issued pistol and brown leather shoulder holster.

———

After calling in the near hit-and-run, Sam and Cici worked their way back to the post office. Cici's skin seemed to pull taut as she clutched at the door handle, waiting for the slam of a large, fast-moving vehicle into theirs.

Nothing happened. No vehicle came close.

Cici sighed with relief as she and Sam climbed from the SUV

and walked toward the entrance's sliding doors. As they entered the large, white atrium, she noticed the parking lot was nearly empty—in large part because it was a mid-week afternoon, no doubt. Cici's heeled sandals clicked over the dirt-tinged tiles and she shivered as she and Sam approached the bank of silver post office boxes. No one else was there. She glanced through the other set of glass doors and saw a line of about eight people waiting with packages. A couple were on their phones, two stared at her through the glass, boredom and irritation mixing in their expressions.

"Which number?" Cici asked, her light voice reverberating around the empty space.

Sam pointed and then handed Cici the key. She held her breath as she inserted the key into the lock. It turned smoothly, and he opened the metal rectangle. The inside was pitch black, and they both bent forward to get a better view.

Cici reached forward just as a loud, high-pitched whine slammed into Cici's ears. She flinched. Sam slammed the box door shut and plastered his back to Cici's front, pressing her tighter against the cold metal behind her as he yanked the key from the lock. With his left hand, he reached across his body and unholstered his gun.

Faster than Cici could catch, Sam pocketed the key and placed both hands on his gun. The sprinklers turned on, soaking them both in a fine sheen of frigid water. Screams and yells came from the other room as people ran out the main sliding doors, their packages now over their heads as water dripped down the boxes and wet T-shirts.

Cici's heart slammed hard against her ribs as the patrons'

curses and shoes thudded through the building puddles.

"Dial 911." Sam's clipped words remained low, his head turning in an active sweep as he sought the unknown target. Was the person escaping with the crowd?

That would be smart.

Cici fumbled her phone out of her pocket, and, bending her head over it as protectively as she could to reduce potential water damage, she placed the call.

"Sh-shots fired," she managed to get past her chattering teeth. "Pacheco p-post office. M-multiple sh-shots."

"We have two units dispatched to your location, Cici. Hold tight. Both you and Sam," Jen, the dispatcher said. "Stay on the line, 'kay? Don't hang up. The cavalry is on its way."

"Should we leave?" Cici asked Sam.

"No," Sam barked. "We're easy targets through the sliding door, and I want to be here, by the box."

"I didn't see anything in it," Cici said.

"It's empty."

12

Conscience doth make cowards of us all.
— Shakespeare

Cici pushed at Sam's back, but the man didn't budge. He outweighed her by a good ninety pounds of muscle and had an additional eight inches in height.

"Why am I standing here, dripping wet, if there's nothing in the box?"

"One. Shut your mouth. I need to hear intruders."

Cici slammed her mouth shut and pressed her cold cheek against Sam's much warmer shoulder blade.

Sirens blared and a trio of police cars sped into the parking lot, their colored lights reverberating off the dingy tiles and metal lockers.

"They're here," Cici said to Jen, who seemed to crumple through the phone.

"Thank goodness," Jen muttered. "Be safe."

Cici clicked off the phone and continued to shiver. Sam waited until the officers entered the building and the sprinklers turned off before turning partially toward her. He kept his gun at his side, pressed against his sodden pant leg.

"Two, I said the box was empty, not that there was nothing

in it," Sam continued as if there hadn't been a long lull in their conversation.

Who did that?

Cici's teeth chattered so hard, her entire body shook.

"There's a difference?" she managed to stutter.

"I hope so."

Sam took in her body-wracking convulsions. Without a word, he holstered his weapon and asked one of the patrolmen to bring in a blanket or jacket or something for her. Cici smiled her thanks when a female officer named Lorena Hammel brought her a dry uniform shirt. She tipped her head back, clenching her jaw against the waves of chills still wracking her body.

"I'll walk with you to the next bank of boxes so you can change out of your wet top," Lorena said.

"That's where the shots came from," Sam said.

"And it's been cleared by two officers," Lorena said. "Back door is unlocked. Perp probably ducked out that way. If he or she didn't run out with the stampede."

Sam frowned even as he nodded.

Cici trotted toward the back of the building, holding the shirt out in front of her to keep it dry. Once in the relative privacy of the space, Cici stripped off her wet blouse and sighed as the dry, if scratchy, polyester slid against her skin. After buttoning the too-large shirt, she bent down to pick up her ruined blouse.

She paused as her eye caught on one of the lower boxes that sat slightly ajar. "Um, Lorena?" Cici asked.

"Yeah?"

Cici pointed to the open door, her hands still shaking, but not with cold.

"Detective Chastain?" Lorena called as she crouched down, peering at the box's door before squinting to see inside.

Sam popped around the bank of metal lockers, eyebrows raised. Lorena gestured toward the box.

"She found it," Lorena said in an accusatory voice. "And I guess she found out why you two were shot at here."

"I can't leave you alone for two minutes, Cee," Sam said on a sigh.

"I'll bag her blouse since she dropped it in front of the locker," Lorena said, already reaching into her back pocket, probably for a freezer bag used for evidence.

She turned to Cici, a faint smile playing on her lips as she bagged up Cici's sodden blouse.

"The detective said you're a good-luck charm. Guess he's right."

"If you think it's good luck to be shot at," Cici grumbled.

Another uniformed patrolman poked his head around the corner.

"Get me a drug-sniffer," Sam said on a sigh. "And we need a camera to document this so I can request a warrant for the entire facility."

Cici stared at the wet, white substance glopping from an opened plastic bag.

———

"That post office box is registered to Donald Johnson," Sam said into the phone.

"Which one?" Cici asked as she cradled her phone between

her shoulder and ear. She set down her coffee mug next to her laptop, barely managing to keep it upright when Mona shoved it with her nose.

"The one you found with your blouse. The other one's *still* registered to Rosalia Sanchez."

"That doesn't make any sense. She's been dead a long time."

"But her husband had to know about it to close it."

"Oh. Don't they just change the lock or whatever if your invoice is overdue?" Cici asked.

"That's the kicker. The bill's all paid up."

"And her husband, Miguel, didn't pay it?"

"Says he didn't know about it."

Cici ran her hands up and down her arms, trying to distill the shivers building there.

"That's creepy, Sam. I don't like this."

Her sermon for this Sunday was coming along about as well as last week's had—which was a problem considering the number of emails and calls she'd fielded about her previous performance. Still, for all that, Cici was glad to be at home, working.

Sam wanted Cici to come back to the station with him, but she'd declined. Cici needed to process what happened today— the gift Anna Carmen offered in the form of a mailbox full of opioids. Why it was open, Cici couldn't guess—except that divine intervention was alive and well.

At least in the form of a spectral Anna Carmen. Cici sent her sister a telepathic hug, but, as was usual when it didn't involve life and death situations, nothing came back.

Cici swallowed hard, wishing for the millionth time that day

Anna Carmen was alive, sitting next to her. She would get such a kick out of Cici working with Sam. For some reason, Anna Carmen liked the idea of Sam and Cici spending time together—and their current successes at policing would have tickled her bright pink with happiness.

When Sam suggested she get a full-time shadow to track her every move, Cici declined that level of personal space invasion. Okay, so not her every move so much as to keep an eye out for the freaky person in black who'd scared her so badly…and who seemed to be running a drug ring out of the post offices in the area.

Her sermon cursor flashed like a tiny beacon of how much Cici had failed at multiple aspects of her life. Like keeping her sister safe and alive.

"True," Sam said. "But we did ask for an autopsy."

What was he talking about? Right, Miguel Sanchez.

Cici lowered her head to the edge of her desk and banged her forehead there. "To see if Donald died from an opioid overdose?"

"Bingo," Sam said. "Though I don't think he did, but we may get the substance in his bloodstream—if we're lucky."

"And the drugs we found were his next shipment?"

"Seems like an educated guess," Sam said. "Lot of 'em, though. Heroin. High-quality from what I heard. You'd make a good investigator, Cee."

"Nope. I hate blood. And getting shot at. And almost dying. How do you handle it?"

Sam was quiet for a long time. "You know how I planned to be a lawyer back in high school?"

Cici made a humming noise in her throat because she was

busy sucking down a big gulp of the latte she needed. Sleep hadn't been easy to wrestle. Her body ached and her chest remained heavy with dread. Even in her own home, thanks to the peek-show two nights ago, Cici struggled to relax.

"I hate the death and pain people cause each other," Sam muttered. "But I can't let it go unchecked. Back then? I thought making money was the most important option. That way I could provide for my family. Even with the death and nasty side of life, I feel like I'm doing work Anna Carmen can be proud of. Hopefully, you, too."

"She would be," Cici said past the lump in her throat. "I'm so proud of you, Sam. Anna Carmen would say the same."

"Good. That matters. Now, I need you to come up to the precinct."

Cici chewed the inside of her cheek. "I'm trying to write my sermon."

"And I need to know you're in one piece."

"You saw me just hours ago."

"C'mon, Cee. Don't argue. Just bring your laptop up here if you think you're really going to get anything accomplished."

"And what about the phone calls or if I'm needed at the hospital?"

"You have a prayer chain and the retired reverend in your congregation—what's his name?"

"Gordon Sommers."

"Right. He's fielding those calls today and tomorrow since you're dealing with a personal issue."

"When did you talk to Carole?"

"'Bout half an hour ago."

"She is scary effective," Cici mused.

"Good thing she's working for God and not the criminals," Sam said.

Cici laughed. "Amen to that."

———

Cici drove her now-cleaned car to the police precinct. She needed to thank Justin for getting her car detailed.

Not that she wanted to be at the precinct. Not that she wanted to realize how deep she'd slid into the ugly underbelly of criminals in less than a week.

Finding Donald on that rock in Santa Fe National Forest opened the wound of losing Anna Carmen, sure, but it also changed Cici's life. Instead of hiking and considering her next sermon, as she normally would, Cici swung her legs back and forth as she leaned back in the curved plastic chair next to Sam's desk.

"Hey, Rev," Justin said as he stuck his head around the corner where Sam's desk sat. Sam positioned it well—away from the hub-bub of the uniformed officer's main bull pen. "Want some coffee? We got us one of those Keurig machines this year. It's bribery for slashing our budget by five percent next fiscal year."

"The city's slashing your budget?" Cici asked. She eyed the coffee with longing but shook her head. "I'm already four cups deep this morning. My legs won't stay still."

Justin's smile curved fully, his eyes lighting up as they landed on her legs. He cleared his throat and met her gaze.

"Well, yeah. The governor swept all agencies and departments, clearing out their rainy-day funds. She's giving back a pittance of the stash and using the rest to fund…who knows what? More drunken pizza parties?"

Cici glanced around, her heart rate speeding up a little more—this time not related to the copious amounts of coffee she drank.

"I thought police folk liked the governor."

Justin raised his brow. "Not when she's slashing our budget and making it harder to keep the community safe."

"I didn't deal with this when I lived in Jamaica Beach."

"Bet your property taxes were a lot higher up there near Boston. So…coffee?"

"Sure," Cici said, giving in to her craving. "Thanks, Justin."

He ambled off—the same slow procession he'd used for all the years she'd known him. That attention to detail made him an exceptional forensic photographer but also made him annoying whenever she tried to play a board game or some pickup softball against him.

"Sorry about that," Sam said, hustling back into the cubby space. "Got some more reports I wanted to go over."

Cici waved her hand. "No worries. Justin stopped in. He's bringing me coffee."

Sam peered at Cici over the white sheets of paper. He dropped his gaze back to the words therein when Justin came in with a Styrofoam cup, steaming with some substance that smelled vaguely coffee-like—but more like the old laundromat on St. Michael's Drive.

Cici tried not to wrinkle her nose as she accepted the cup with a smile.

"Got anything to help you figure out who's dealing the drugs through the post offices all over the state?" Justin asked.

"I'm not sure we have a drug ring being run through post offices," Sam said, not bothering to look up.

"Huh. I heard from my buddy you were talking to the sheriff's department down in Madrid about that."

"I went to Madrid last week to get a gift for Jeannette. Met up with Cici at a café. Had a drink."

Justin gripped the back of Cici's chair. Sam still didn't look up, which made Cici's legs bounce faster. Her stomach began to ache from the tension rising in this small corner of the building. Sam wasn't sharing his information with Justin. In fact, he'd just *lied* to another member of the police force about his activities.

"You didn't tell me that," Justin murmured into Cici's ear.

"A lot has happened since then," Cici said.

Justin straightened.

Sam continued to peruse his papers.

She picked up her cup and brought it to her mouth, but her stomach rebelled and she was unable to take a sip.

Sam's phone rang and he answered it with a gruff, "Chastain." He listened for a moment, his cheeks going slack before his lips firmed. "Two? Both? Just one. Where? Got it."

He hung up as his scowl blackened. "Let's go, Cee. Seems we have two more folks with the same signature."

"I'll come with you," Justin said.

Sam's shoulders tensed but he kept walking.

"Why do you say that?" Cici asked as she trotted after Justin and Sam, trying to keep up with their longer strides.

"Signature?" Justin asked. "Because that's what it is."

"What does that mean?"

Neither man answered her.

Cici sighed. "Where are we going?"

"New Presby hospital," Sam said over his shoulder.

"Um…why?" Cici replied, picking up her pace to a trot.

"Because we have a potential overdose from opioids and a stab wound," Sam said. He glanced back and caught the look on Cici's face. "No one was dead when we got the call," Sam continued, his voice gentling.

"Narcan administered?" Justin asked.

"Dunno."

"You want pictures of the survivor?" Justin slid into the front passenger seat and Sam into the driver's seat of Sam's city-designated sedan. Thank goodness it wasn't a typical police car because then Cici would have to sit in the back in "the cage," as the officers called it. Now that would be embarrassing for a reverend—pictures of her in the prisoner section would be all over social media and possibly the Santa Fe New Mexican. Not the kind of press she needed, even if her church was young and growing.

Sam slowed down for the light at Camino Carlos Rey. He glanced back at her in the rearview mirror before refocusing on the road. What was with the constant looks? Did he expect her to disappear?

Sure, Anna Carmen pretty much fell off Sam's radar for those last couple of years, which probably accounted for why Cici and Sam began to talk more consistently and plan to get together when they were both in Santa Fe—an uncommon occurrence what with Cici finishing her master's. But, by then, Anna Carmen had been deep into a relationship with Evan, and between spending time with him and her demanding work schedule, she rarely spent time with Sam.

The realization made Cici start. Anna Carmen told her the Monday of the week of her death that she expected Evan to propose. In all of their conversations within six months before her death, she'd talked Cici's ear off about her grand wedding plans.

If that relationship was going to wedding bells, then…well, it was time to visit slick lawyer Evan once again and find out what he was hiding about Anna Carmen. Because the man should know more than he'd told her.

Especially now that Evan told Cici her twin was spending time right before her death with none other than Donald Johnson—a married man—and potential opioid-addict. Both women developed strong opinions about marriage and monogamy when the girls' father cheated on their mother, the last time with a wealthy widow, KaraLynn. Fifteen years Frank Gurule's senior, the elegant woman promised to open doors for Frank professionally and politically.

KaraLynn had, and Cici's family fell apart.

Which made Anna Carmen's time with Donald even stranger.

"Before she died, was Anna Carmen happy with Evan?" she asked.

Sam turned onto St. Michael's. His hand clutched the steering wheel tight enough for his knuckles to turn white.

Not a good sign, especially from the man who'd been Anna Carmen's best friend. But Cici had long suspected there was more going on between Sam and her twin than just shared interests and senses of humor.

Maybe the paradise Cici had heard about Anna Carmen and Evan every other day—most every day—back then was a lie, like the partial truths Cici told Anna Carmen about her relationship with Lyndon.

Maybe it had been concocted so that Anna Carmen had something interesting to tell Cici next time they spoke. Something as fascinating as the life Cici embellished for her sister living in the hometown she grew up in, unable to think of something else to pass the unending evening hours.

"She and Evan seemed pretty cozy," Justin said, craning his neck back to look at her. "Why?"

Cici shrugged. For some reason, she refused to delve deeper into her sister's personal life right now. Sam's hand eased on the wheel.

When they arrived at the hospital, Cici stumbled to a halt to find Carole in the waiting room, comforting Juan and another teenager—Jaycee. Justin hovered in the doorway as Cici and Sam hurried into the room.

"We're so glad you came," Juan said, almost bowling Cici over as he hugged her in his big arms.

She patted his back as best she could with her arms pinioned to her side. Her wide eyes sought Carole's, who dipped her head toward Juan. Cici closed her eyes as the pain of what she'd hear next began to rip through her.

"How's your father, Juan?" she asked.

He sniffled and stepped back. Cici blinked in surprise at the big grin that lit up the young man's face.

"He's doing okay. Dr. Van der Veen expects a full recovery."

"Wow," Cici whispered, shocked. "Really?" Cici's voice grew stronger and this time she launched herself at Juan. "That's the best news."

"Yeah, I know." Juan blew out a breath. "But I don't get it. My dad isn't into drugs. If Jaycee hadn't found him…"

Juan inclined his head toward the girl with long reddish blond hair who'd stood from her seat, looking nervous.

"Blessings, Jaycee. I'm so glad you were able to help Mr. Sanchez."

"Me, too," she said in a soft voice. "If I'd come over later, it might've been too late."

"A happy accident you arrived when you did," Carole said, coming to join the group. "Me, too, really. I'd just dropped off some chile at the Durants across the road when Jaycee came out of the house, shrieking."

Jaycee dropped her eyes to her scuffed boots, clearly not liking the reminder of how she'd initially handled the crisis.

"I thought you said something about two people," Cici said to Sam.

He shrugged.

Justin clapped Juan on the shoulder. "Really glad your pop pulled through, man."

"So, who's the other person here, then?" Cici asked, still trying to get her bearings.

"Oh. Um," Carole backed up, her lips compressing in a thin line.

Cici turned toward Sam, who stood uncharacteristically quiet. He shuffled his feet and didn't want to answer her question. Cici turned toward Justin.

"I don't know," he said with a shrug. "I came along to document." He lifted his camera.

"Susan Johnson," Sam said, his voice clipped.

What was his problem?

"Donald's wife, Susan?" Cici asked, her stomach hitting some place too low for a body to hold all the organs.

"Yeah. She's…well…it's not drugs."

"Oh?" Cici asked, confusion and worry warring in her chest.

"She was…she was found next to Miguel's car."

Cici's eyes sought Juan's, and the boy stared back in stony silence.

"Did you know about them? I mean, were Susan and your dad an item?"

Juan shook his head. "None of that makes sense. None of it." Juan's voice shook. "My dad doesn't like Donald Johnson or his wife. Calls 'em snooty gringos."

Not unusual for the locals to say about incoming wealthier Caucasians, especially the Texas and California transplants.

"He would never be caught near Mrs. Johnson, Rev. And he'd never shoot up. Not after it killed Marco."

"What are you saying, Juan?" Sam asked.

Juan glanced at Cici, probably trying to figure out if she'd shared the information he'd given her the other day with the other adults here.

"No way my dad took heroin, Detective Chastain," Juan said, his eyes pleading. "*No way*. He'd lose his job." Justin's eyes narrowed as he focused on the wall across the waiting room. "Still might," he mumbled.

Cici gripped his hand. "I'm here for you, Juan. For your father and grandmother. I'm happy to talk to your father's boss. Whatever you need."

"Coming to see you was a big mistake, Rev," Juan said. He scrubbed his palms over his eyes, causing them to look even more bloodshot when he dropped his large hands.

"Come on, Juan," Jaycee said, still unable to meet any of the adult's eyes. "You need to walk a bit."

"But…"

"Come on," she gritted, tugging his arm. Her eyes skittered toward Justin before landing back on the floor.

She and Miguel disappeared down the hallway, his head bent down to whatever she whispered in his ear.

13

Presume not that I am the thing I was.
— Shakespeare

Cici turned to Carole. "Will you please notify our congregation that we have two members in the hospital? I'll stay here until I speak to both."

Carole looked like she wanted to argue, but she just sighed before she dipped her head in a brief nod.

"You'll make sure she gets some rest?" Carole asked Sam. "Last time we had someone in the hospital, Cici didn't leave for two full days."

"Sure," Sam said.

"All right. I'll do that before I go to my evening yoga."

"You sure we want her as an assistant?" Justin muttered after Carole left the room.

Cici swung toward him, shocked by his words. "What's that supposed to mean?"

Justin crossed his arms over his chest, gaze still on the door where Carole exited. "She's...bossy."

Cici mimicked his stance. "She's also organized and gets tons of stuff done, which is why we're able to function with just the two of us on staff full-time."

"Doesn't make her any nicer," Justin muttered again as he turned toward the lobby. "Since you don't need any photo documentation, I'll get a ride back to the precinct," he called over his shoulder to Sam.

He sauntered down the hall, following Carole and the kids.

Cici and Sam settled back into the chairs and waited.

———

Sam had an issue with a warrant he wanted to pursue, related to Donald Johnson's properties—though Cici was unclear as to what the problem was exactly. Something about another ongoing investigation, she decided. When she asked, Sam chose not to answer her question, probably because Carole returned with Juan and Jaycee in tow.

A few minutes later, Susan awoke.

"Thank goodness for my silver belt," she said with a nod toward the thick-disked-chain. One of the links appeared bent and covered in dried blood.

Cici took her shaking hand and squeezed gently, noting Susan must have been stabbed in the back. *In the back.* Like Donald, like Anna Carmen. Cici forced her fingers open, releasing Susan's when the older woman winced.

"Miguel Sanchez didn't stab me, Cici," Susan said, her voice low but her eyes alert. They scanned the room, paying special attention to the doorway behind Cici's chair.

"Why do you say that?"

Susan had the grace to blush. "One, I waited until Miguel was inside to go over to his car."

"You sure he didn't come back out?" Cici asked.

"Yes, and I smelled perfume. I was turning, anyway, because Miguel locked the car and I couldn't get into it." She scrunched her eyebrows, dissatisfied with the turn of events. "I've smelled it before, the perfume," she murmured.

"I have some questions about you trying to enter Miguel Sanchez's vehicle, Mrs. Johnson," Sam said.

"I'm sure you do. I'll answer them."

"You're sure you smelled perfume?"

"One hundred percent. I wish I'd heard the voice of the woman who called in, pretending to be me the day Donnie died." She sighed, closing her eyes as tears leaked out. "Maybe I was too quick to judge." She opened her eyes. "Maybe he did love me?"

Cici cradled the older woman's hands in hers again. "He looked at you with devotion."

Susan sniffled then grimaced. She glanced up toward the doorway where Carole hovered, holding a large bouquet of flowers.

"I was on my way out when a nurse signed for these for you," Carole said. "I offered to bring them up so you could enjoy them now."

"I wanted you to know," Susan said, her voice quiet, "I've talked to J.R. and changed my will. If something happens to me, my estate goes to your church."

Cici blinked, the shock coating her skin. "But…"

Susan smirked a little. "I'm hoping it's incentive to keep me alive until I come to my senses and spend all that glorious cash on amazing trips and expensive whiskey. I do like whiskey."

"I don't want your money, Susan. I want your shining face

in my congregation." Cici waved Carole in. She settled the large bouquet of flowers on a small nightstand.

"How are you feeling?" Carole asked.

"Like I was stabbed in the back," Susan replied. "Probably J.R. sent those. He's been so good about checking up on me. Since Donnie's death."

"I'll let the church members know you're awake." Carole bustled from the room.

"Why were you trying to break into Miguel Sanchez's car?" Sam asked.

Susan's face lost color and she focused on the blanket near her hand.

"Susan," Cici said. "That's—"

"Necessary when you see a strange person inside the car at five in the morning," Susan snapped. "Just after Miguel went in and to bed. And, no, I don't have a description. It was still fairly dark and the person wore dark clothes and one of those beanie hats the kids prefer these days."

Susan's final words sounded defensive. Cici glanced up to see how Sam was reacting to this information, but he had on his detective face and she couldn't read his expression.

Cici rested her hip on the edge of the bed. "Why don't you tell me?"

"I found a key and some…what I suppose are drugs. Some white pills in a little bag. They were under the car. Near the driver's side door."

"Where are they now?" Cici asked.

"I have no idea. I got stabbed before I managed to pick them up."

"It was a warning," Susan said, her voice holding a raspy edge of fear. "To keep my nose out of Donnie's death. I think…I think that's why that woman called in Donnie's death. So I'd think the worst of my husband."

"Good thing Juan's dogs scared off your attacker," Sam said. "You're very lucky your wound isn't worse."

Susan scowled but inclined her head.

"Want to tell me why you don't like Juan?" Sam asked, his voice gentle.

"I'm just not much of a fan of men who threaten my husband or me," Susan said, her voice and body stiffly upright.

"When did that happen?" I asked.

"Before you came to start the church, dear. He told me I was a rich *gringa* who didn't know half of what my husband had been involved in. Like he could have dirt on Donnie."

Sam and Cici locked gazes and an understanding passed between them.

"Did he?" Sam asked.

"Yes," Susan snapped.

"What was it he thought he knew?" Cici asked, her voice softer.

Susan huffed. "I'd rather not…I don't want to talk about it."

"Susan," Cici started.

"I'm tired and need to rest. Please." Her lip quivered and her eyes filled with tears. Cici grabbed a few tissues and offered them to Susan.

"You'd tell me if you thought it would help the case?" Sam asked. "I don't want to postpone your trip, but you need to be honest with me. You've been stabbed. Miguel is full of heroin and

Narcan. Donald's dead, as is Anna Carmen and Miguel's son and wife. We've lost a lot of people to this killer. I don't want to lose anyone else."

Susan dabbed her eyes with one of the tissues. It turned black with mascara. She wadded it into a ball, her hand fisting around it.

"Oh, fine," Susan said. "He'd go to the prison. Once a week. He visited Ernesto Espinoza."

"I know that name," Cici said, her brow wrinkling as she tried to remember a face, a connection.

"Justin's uncle," Sam said. He didn't look happy. Nope, not with the way his eyes blazed and his lips compressed. Whatever else Sam knew about this Ernesto was not good.

"He's in jail?" Cici asked, shocked.

Sam began to pace the small confines of the room. "Was. Federal prison. For drug trafficking."

Yeah, not good. Cici settled on the edge of the hard hospital mattress.

"He was supposed to get out around the time your...," Susan said, her voice quiet as if she was admitting to a sin. Perhaps she was. She looked down at her lap and shredded the tissue. "He left the prison a year and a half ago. I'd say within a week, maybe two of when Rosalia Sanchez died."

"Who picked Ernesto up from the prison, Susan?" Sam's voice was coaxing but also full of authority.

A thrill shot through Cici. This was Sam at work. At his best. He wanted to solve this crime—to stop more unnecessary deaths, of course, but because the evidence would lead to who killed Anna Carmen.

It would lead to justice.

Cici struggled to focus around the thick, heavy weight of grief and regret that wrapped around her. She'd thought justice would bring peace.

It wouldn't because Anna Carmen would still be dead.

Susan no longer tried to swipe at the tears and mascara running down her face. "Donnie picked him up. Brought him into town."

"Miguel thinks he murdered Rosalia?" Sam asked.

"He doesn't think," Susan muttered, obviously miserable. "He says he *knows*. Ernesto told him."

14

Men should be what they seem. — *Shakespeare*

"Why?" Sam asked, finally coming to a stop right next to Susan's bedside.

"Donnie was his—Ernesto's—lawyer. He delivered the sealed envelope to Miguel."

"Why didn't Miguel press charges?"

Susan's face crumpled further. "He wanted to. But then…then his son died. And Anna Carmen died just a week later."

"Hush killings," Sam growled.

"What?" Cici asked, her head seeming to float a full second behind her ears.

Whatever Sam meant by that upset him. He rose, his body taut, his face set in unforgiving lines. Susan peeked up at him but dropped her gaze back to her lap.

"But…but he's dead now. Ernesto," Susan whispered as she wiped her eyes. "He died in a boating accident off the coast of Cabo."

Sam made a deep guttural sound in his throat. This was the information he'd wanted to bring Anna Carmen's killer to light. To have the person be dead…

Even for Cici, who hadn't spent so much of the last year dedicated to this aspect of her sister's murder, the information Susan provided was anticlimactic. Wrong.

"Before you ask, yes, I'm sure it was Ernesto. He was identified. And he left all his money, everything, to his wife. None of that money came back stateside."

"How can you be sure?"

Susan opened her mouth. Shut it and frowned. "I guess...I guess I can't. But Justin is Ernesto's only living relative, and he doesn't have any money. He works for the police, for God's sakes."

Like working for the police equated to menial labor. Cici guessed when you amassed the kind of wealth Susan enjoyed, police work did seem menial.

Cici made herself a promise—well, more of a reiteration of a promise: she would never, ever consider hardworking people beneath her.

"But the drug ring didn't end," Sam said.

Susan shook her head. "I guess not."

"Susan," Sam said, his voice holding an edge that sounded dangerous. He looked collected except for the tautness of his shoulder—the strain in his neck muscles. "Be straight with me now. This is information you've withheld for over a year. Enough for us to have solved this crime then." He didn't say the phrase but it seemed to float around the room: obstruction of justice.

"I tried to stay out of Donnie's dealings. I just wanted the security of our lifestyle."

Sam scooted closer, but it was Cici who spoke. Her voice was shrill and just as sharp as Sam's had been. "My sister died. You knew who did it. Or at least who was involved. You and Donald should have stepped forward, should have made sure no one else had to suffer like me, like Miguel and Juan." Cici dropped her voice. "Like you're hurting now. We've all hurt like that. It'll hurt forever when someone in your family's murdered. All the way to your soul."

Susan gripped the sheets, her knuckles white. "I didn't know then." She raised her wet, red eyes to Cici's. "I didn't know."

More like she didn't *want* to know. Cici crossed her arms over her chest as she tried to hold in the pain from Susan's revelations.

"Donnie didn't tell me. But he was upset. Real upset. Then, a few months ago, he seemed better."

"Why?" Sam asked.

"I don't know," Susan leaned back against the pillows, her eyes heavy and her face slackening with fatigue. "He didn't tell me."

"Fine," Sam said, but his voice said it wasn't. "What about Anna Carmen? She came to see Donald."

"She knew Marco didn't…didn't overdose," Susan whispered. "That young man was murdered."

Cici couldn't breathe. Killing a teenaged boy. Killing her sister. To keep Miguel silent?

"A child? Whoever…killed a *child*?"

15

Hell is empty and all the devils are here.
— Shakespeare

Cici couldn't breathe. Sam touched the back of her hand with two fingers—just a brief sweep, but it helped her focus.

"I'll check the drug. I bet it's the same one they gave Miguel. Or same signature in his blood stream," Sam said. "We have the pathology report for Marco on file."

Sam scrubbed his palms over his face and into his hair. He looked up at the ceiling. Silence built.

"I'm going to need you to sign an affidavit," Sam warned. "I need this in writing."

Susan collapsed deeper into the bed, yelped when her stitches pulled. Cici took a step toward her, then paused. All this time, Susan knew details about the person who killed Anna Carmen. She *knew* and said nothing.

Donald knew—an elder of her church, one of the founding members—and worked for and released the man who killed her sister.

Cici turned on her heel, unable even to look at the woman again. She needed to scream. She needed to keep screaming and…and…*hit* something. Instead, Cici stalked out of the room.

She put one foot in front of the other. When she slammed into a person—large, white coat, probably a doctor—she leaned against the wall and shut her eyes. But her knees didn't want to support her now that she'd wobbled. She slid down and let her forehead fall forward onto her thighs.

The tears of loss burned up her throat, burned her nose, but her eyes remained dry.

Someone settled on the ground next to her. The scent of Sam's soap tickled her nose, settled some of the fury and grief roiling through her.

"You think it's true?" Cici gasped, trying not to break the last restraints. If she cried now, she might not stop. Ever.

Aci.

Their mother kept a picture of the two of them on the refrigerator. The babies were less than a day old, holding hands. Anna Carmen had always been Cici's best friend.

Part of her died that day, with Anna Carmen. Cici didn't have words to explain the phenomenon, but when Anna Carmen's consciousness faded, so did part of Cici's.

Sam pulled her into his embrace, his large palm encircling much of her shoulder. "I don't know. It's a convenient explanation."

Cici lifted her head. "Why is it convenient?" she cried. "My sister *died.*"

Sam pulled her even tighter into his embrace. "Because we can't touch Ernesto Espinoza. He's allegedly dead. And as a drug trafficker, he'd have the ability to silence people."

"But…," Cici said, searching Sam's troubled eyes.

"But…it's so *clean*, Cee. And it doesn't explain now. I mean, this week. Who took over, why kill Donald. Who attempted to stab Susan?"

"Maybe Miguel did," Cici muttered.

"You think that? Really?"

Cici dropped her gaze back to the linoleum between her spread legs. "No," she said after another long moment of silence. "I don't. But…why would Susan lie?"

Sam stood and pulled Cici to her feet. "We pushed her for an answer. She was scared."

At least this newfound rage swept away the urge to cry. "Of what?"

Sam kept hold of Cici's chilled hand as he tugged her back toward Susan's room. "Not what. Who."

Sam didn't seem surprised that Susan no longer occupied the space. He glanced around the room, his eyes landing on the flowers. He searched them for a card, but there wasn't one.

Sam dug deeper into the flowers. He cursed, low and vicious.

He pulled something buried deep between the foliage.

"What's that?" Cici asked, mesmerized by the small bits of wire.

"Transmitter." He dug further. He pulled out a tiny microphone.

———

Sam yanked Cici down the hallway, barking questions at the nurses and other medical staff. None had seen Susan Johnson— or would admit to seeing her leave.

After another call to the station where Sam patiently went over the situation not once, but twice, a uniformed officer showed up to escort Cici home.

"Go on with Kevin," Sam said. "I'm going to be tied up here for a while."

"But…" Cici looked around. The hospital room now crawled with the forensics team. Justin snapped pictures on the far side.

"What about Susan?" Cici asked.

"I have an APB on her, an officer out front of her house. Best thing you can do, Cee, is let me do my job. And do *not*, under any circumstance, go to Susan's house or warn the Sanchezes."

"But…" Cici huffed a breath.

"Any circumstance," Sam repeated, his eyes narrowed and angry.

"All right. I'm ready to go, Officer Loomis."

Kevin escorted her from the building, sticking closer to Cici's side than allowed her to be comfortable. But she didn't question him. At least she had a trained professional there with her who'd try to keep her safe.

"Sam'll go by the state pen, I bet," Kevin Loomis rumbled.

"Why would he do that?" Cici asked.

"To cover all his bases. Sam's real good at his job."

Cici turned to stare out the car window. She didn't understand how mortal enemies like Donald Johnson and Miguel Sanchez could sit in nearby pews each Sunday.

Nothing she considered, no way she looked at that problem made sense.

When they arrived at Cici's place, Kevin, her current babysitter, said he'd stay in his car to keep watch. Once she locked her door and looked out the window at him, she shook her head as he bent his head over his phone.

After wandering through the house for a few minutes, Cici sat back down at her computer that she'd picked up from the police station, pulling her sermon notes closer.

The intense heat broke as low, thick, gray clouds rolled in over the mountains. The air sizzled with ozone. An early-afternoon thunderstorm quenched the hungry land's thirst and caused Cici to jump at each of the rumbles of thunder.

After another hour spent on forums and leafing through her large, worn family Bible, Cici shut the book and drained the dregs of her second latte. She didn't even shudder at its icy temperature nor did she focus on her still-empty document that was supposed to hold this week's sermon.

She walked to her room and changed into her hiking shorts and boots.

"All right, you two," she said to her dogs. "Let's walk."

Cici pulled up Sam's last text and let him know she'd be on the Dale Ball trail system. *Not too far. I know it's getting late.* He didn't text her back, probably because he was interrogating one of her parishioners.

That's the part Cici hated—that more of her churchgoers were being pulled into this insidious web. She couldn't sit here and just…well, wait.

The dogs needed to move. So did Cici. She wanted to run and never stop.

Since she couldn't do that, she'd settled for a strenuous hike with her dogs.

After ensuring she had enough water for all three of them, she clipped the dog's leashes to their harnesses and loaded them in the car. Kevin Loomis wandered over.

She let him know her plans. He looked unhappy.

"Sam said for you to stay home," Kevin said.

"I can't." The keys jingled in Cici's hand. "I won't go far, but I need…" The dogs tugged at their leashes, slamming into each other. "I'll be with my dogs. You can come, too."

Those were the best concessions Cici could make.

Still, Kevin tried to get in touch with Sam. He didn't answer, so Kevin reluctantly agreed. Cici drove to the trail turnout, and Kevin followed at a respectable distance. Once parked, Cici shoved in her earbuds before unloading the dogs in a flurry of happy barks and plumed tails.

"Coming?" Cici asked.

Kevin looked around. He shook his head but went to stand near the trail head. "Not too far," he warned.

Cici nodded.

They headed up the trail while old grunge pounded into Cici's ears. Not quite God' music, but it was Anna Carmen's favorite and it suited her mood.

They rounded the mile marker, and Cici's body was slicked in sweat and her breath puffed from her parted lips thanks to the punishing pace she'd set. She stopped to slug back water from her canteen.

In that moment, between one song and the next, Cici's neck iced, as though frigid fingers slid across it. Without conscious thought, she dropped to the ground while Mona and Rodolfo stiffened, eyes facing down the trail, growling. The dogs' hackles rose as they lunged toward a stand of trees to Cici's left. She yanked the earbuds from her ears, just able to make out the quick patter of running shoes on the trail through that copse.

16

I had rather hear my dog bark at a crow, than a
man swear he loves me. — Shakespeare

Rodolfo bared his teeth with a deep snarl. Mona hung back, closer to Cici, who laid her free hand—the one not struggling to maintain control of the leashes—against the dog's side. With a mighty tug, Rodolfo pulled his leash from where it was wrapped around Cici's other wrist and darted into the trees, leash bumping and dragging behind him.

Cici stood on shaking feet, her breath too short to call for her dog. Mona remained pressed to her leg, shoulder fur ridged and sharp canines visible.

Cici glanced behind her, where a faint outline glowed between piñons.

"Anna Carmen." The name tumbled from Cici's lips, catching almost on a sob.

Cici blinked and the apparition disappeared—if it had ever been there to begin with. Cici gaped at the arrow embedded deep in the sappy bark of the tree, just about the height of her head, where Anna Carmen had been.

Mona stayed close to her side as Cici shuffled closer to the arrow. A piece of paper rattled on its shaft, loosened, no doubt, by the force of hitting the tree.

Cici grabbed at the narrow sheaf of paper as it caught another draft of wind. She slid her free hand into Mona's thick, warm coat as she read:

Susan's story wasn't complete fabrication. Evan knew this. Your sister's death didn't have to happen. Evan knew this, too.

Neither does yours.

Typed, like the last one. Just black pixels on white printer paper. Words that sent chills sweeping down Cici's back and curling around her organs.

Cici grappled with her pocket and managed to yank out her phone. Her hands shook but she snapped the picture and texted it to Sam along with the message: *I'm in one piece. Rodolfo took off after someone on the trail.*

Sam's response this time was instantaneous: *Find cover. Sit tight. I'm on my way.*

Much as Cici wanted to argue, she knew Sam's directive was the most prudent.

So, she gripped Mona's leash tighter and settled into the cluster of pine trees not far from the path.

Nearly an hour passed and Cici continued to stare out toward the trail, wishing Rodolfo would trot into the clearing.

He didn't. But Sam did, followed by Justin and Kevin.

"Cici!" Sam bellowed.

"Here," she responded, her voice ragged and too soft. She'd spent this time wishing she'd never left home—that she'd listened to Sam.

That she'd taken these threats with the dead seriousness they required. And wishing her dog returned.

Each moment proved harder to wait out.

Sam turned and homed in on her location.

She managed to stand and dust the pine needles from the seat of her jeans before Sam reached her. He gripped her biceps and turned her first to the right, then the left, to ensure she remained unharmed.

"I'm all right. But Rodolfo never came back."

"Cee," he began. Pain seeped into his eyes. He was the one who had helped her track down the pups after Anna Carmen had died.

When she'd returned to Santa Fe after subleasing her apartment in Boston and resigning from her position at the church, her father had already sold or given away Anna Carmen's life, including her sister's dog. The only reason Cici had the motorcycle was because Sam stored it in his garage—the place Anna Carmen and he used to work on it together.

With Sam's help, Cici tracked Great Pyrenees in the Southwest, looking for the offspring of Anna Carmen's dog, who'd been pregnant when her father had given the dog to a rancher north of Taos.

Mona and Rodolfo were the pups of Anna Carmen's dog, Gidget, now long-dead. Mauled by a black bear while guarding the livestock on the ranch.

"Rodolfo?" she managed to push out.

Sam's lips compressed and his fingers tightened around her forearm, keeping her upright. Cici pressed her free hand to her mouth.

"He's alive," Sam rushed out.

"Your dog's been shot," Justin said, coming up to her other

side. "With an arrow. We called it in on our way up here."

"Great job at screwing that up," Sam muttered as Cici slid from Sam's grip back to the ground.

"Will he...will he make it?" Cici whispered.

She looked between Sam's stoic face and Justin's ashen one. Justin must have just remembered her dogs were the last animated link Cici had to her twin.

"Um," Justin managed.

"Will this stop?" Cici asked. "Will the deaths, the pain—will it stop?"

Sam simply watched her, his eyes as shattered as hers must be.

For the first time since her sister's death—the second time in her life—Cici questioned not just her purpose for being here, but what type of god would allow this much pain.

17

*When sorrows come, they come not single spies. But
in battalions! — Shakespeare*

Cici didn't want to go home, but she didn't have another option, really. She stood, looking up at her front porch. Sam would be back soon. Kevin was parked in her driveway.

If only she'd never left…

"Rev?" The voice was small but it startled Cici.

She dropped her to-go box holding the rest of her dinner on the porch with a thud, her now-empty hands coming to her chest as she breathed through the fright.

"Jaycee. You scared me." Cici bent to pick up the food container, frowning at the seepage both from the eco-friendly packaging and from the new scrapes on her hands.

She was so tired. She closed her eyes, but all she could see was Rodolfo's light brown eyes clouded with pain. The vet allowed Mona to stay in Rodolfo's kennel because the larger dog's vitals ticked better with his sister nosing him.

Her house was dark, too quiet. For the first time, it wasn't a sanctuary she wanted to enter. Not after the person at the window, the truck at her door…the notes. Cici shuddered.

Sam had been sweet to buy her dinner, but Cici wasn't

hungry. Wasn't sure how she'd ever be hungry again now that she had an idea of what got her sister murdered…and how involved the community appeared to be in the cover-up.

Jaycee also looked at the lid. "Sorry about that. I just…I needed to tell you something. About…about Juan's dad. And…and Mrs. Johnson."

Cici locked her knees and her jaw to reduce her trembling. Didn't work. Adrenaline ricocheted through her system, causing her to twitch and gasp.

She cleared her throat, hoping to sound normal. "Come on in and we can talk."

Jaycee stepped farther back into the shadows off to the side of Cici's house.

"No offense, but being seen with you, going in your house… that's why Juan's family's being targeted, Rev. Someone's watching you. And they'll know if I go in."

After her dog getting shot with an arrow…after Miguel's trip to the hospital, there was no way Cici could argue that point. She didn't try.

Cici collapsed into the Adirondack chair next to her front door but had the sense to stare straight out into the street.

"That better?" Cici asked.

"I hope so." Jaycee's voice was soft.

"What did you want to tell me?"

"Juan's dad still had a needle in his arm, Rev."

Cici sat up straighter, but she immediately slumped back onto her seat, trying to look nonchalant. "You're telling me you think someone shot him up intentionally. To silence—no, to kill him?"

"They gave him a lot of something related to opioids, Rev. I know that because that antidote worked. But, Rev, there was a note." A piece of paper fluttered to the porch, landing inches from Cici's foot.

"A note where?" Cici asked.

"Pinned to Miguel's pillow. On the bed."

Cici gripped the edge of the chair, trying hard not to wince when her wounds opened up. "And you took it?"

"Yeah."

"Why would you do that? It's evidence."

"I think you should read it, Rev. And I think you need to be real, *real* careful."

Not that she needed that reminder. All she had to do was look down at her ragged flesh on her hands and arms to know stuff was getting to be more than she could handle—and fast. Her dog, her baby. No, she couldn't fall apart. She would not. Earlier, Crying instead of rushing to his side had almost cost Rodolfo his life.

Cici began to turn but Jaycee made a low sound in her throat. Cici instead bent down and scratched her ankle. She picked up the paper.

"One more thing, Rev. Juan's dad has *never* touched any substance. Not a one. I know Juan told you that, but it's important. And when Juan left to go to work, his dad was sleeping. He'd worked the night shift." Miguel was a prison guard out at the state penitentiary on NM-14.

"All right. That's a lot of information. Why didn't you tell that to Detective Chastain earlier today?"

"Because of who else was there," Jaycee's voice trembled but the words were clear.

Cici continued to stare down at her shoes, but her mind revved and turned over.

"Read the note, Rev."

"What's going on, Jaycee? I don't understand. From what you've said, you think someone came into Juan's house and shot his father up with the drug?"

Jaycee shuffled back, even farther into the shadows. "I don't think that. I *know* it."

"Why?"

"Read the note."

"Fine. Who was there—at the hospital that worried you so much?"

"Justin Espinoza was pulling away from the curb of Juan's house when I turned onto the street," Jaycee muttered.

This time, Cici couldn't stop her head from turning. She wanted to gauge the girl's eyes, see if she was lying. But Jaycee had already melted back into the shadows completely.

Cici unfolded the note with shaking hands.

These words, too, were on printer paper, stark black marks on the otherwise pristine white page.

If you don't stop looking for answers, they're all going to die.

18

These violent delights have violent ends.
— Shakespeare

Nothing upsetting about that note.

Nothing at all.

She had no idea how long she sat there on her porch—exposed to the killer. The words on the page jumped out, retreated.

Shock. She must be in shock.

Finally, Kevin Loomis opened his car door. Cici squinted as the dim light from the door nearly blinded her. She hadn't realized how dark it was—how late and quiet.

"You all right over there, Rev?"

No. She wasn't. Someone planned to kill her. Someone had tried to kill her already—multiple times.

"Yeah," she responded.

She stumbled back into her house where she tossed her leftovers into her trash can. All the while, the note remained clutched in her hand.

She turned the note's warning over in her mind, unsure how to proceed.

She curled onto her couch and pulled out her phone.

"Shock and the aftermath of adrenaline," she mumbled, fumbling with her phone, trying to unlock the screen to call Sam. But already the blackness tugged at her consciousness, pulling her under its thick, opaque wave.

The dream slammed into her with the force of a fist. She stood, once again, at the edge of the road leading to the Santuario de Chimayó.

But, again, in this dream, Cici was Anna Carmen. This time, though, Cici understood Anna Carmen's thoughts, not just her strong emotions.

Weird.

And wrong.

Stay, Anna Carmen whispered into her head. *Stay. You need to see. You must understand.*

Somehow, Cici knew the day to be Good Friday, the day of the Pilgrimage from Santa Fe to the Medina-family chapel next door to the main church that housed the Santo Niño de Atocha—the Christ child—who'd been hailed as the savior of nearly one thousand New Mexico National Guardsmen who'd fought in the Philippines during World War II.

Cici settled into Anna Carmen's consciousness, into her body.

Anna Carmen had made the pilgrimage to clear her head and focus on Evan's proposal. He wanted to marry her, but then he wanted to move immediately to Scottsdale.

Evan had been offered a position with a firm there—a partnership-track where he'd work even longer hours than he did now. Evan didn't want to focus on the trivial cases here. He wanted out of Santa Fe, out of the confinement of a tiny state with few big trials to litigate.

Her phone vibrated in her pocket. That would most likely be Evan, wondering when she'd get to the restaurant—why she hadn't agreed to his rushed proposal or been more excited to leave the mess she'd created with the Sanchez family behind. She stared down at the dusty gray riverbed below her as she ignored the next vibrations and the next.

She tugged her soft fleece jacket tighter around her body.

She should call Cici, talk it through with her sister. Cee asked her yesterday what was bothering her, but she hadn't wanted to pull her sister into the web of conspiracy and half-truths she'd been forced to concoct. Not even Sam or Evan knew how deep she'd wiggled herself down this rabbit hole.

Well, Evan had a good idea, and he was worried. That's why she couldn't tell him anything more until Mr. Sanchez came forward.

But Miguel Sanchez refused to look at the photos Anna Carmen took, shutting the door of his mother's home in her face. Maybe he was right to do so—Marco's death lashed them both.

That poor family—that poor man. To lose a wife and a child in such a short time. That's why she had to do something.

Had she gotten through to Mr. Sanchez? Would the man talk to Evan or the police as she'd suggested? Would the SFPD be able to help protect him and his younger son from the potential backlash from the others involved in the drug ring?

She was so deep in thought, she never heard the other person approach. Only the soft, low voice in her ear. "Thought you'd get away that easy, huh?"

A voice that sounded just like…

———

Cici woke with a start, gasping, her heart pounding an unnatural, heavy rhythm in her chest.

She and her twin were always close but she'd never been *in* Anna Carmen's consciousness before—not that intimately, not feeling her every emotion, knowing her every thought.

Cici pressed her clammy cheeks between her raised knees.

"You're showing me this now?" Cici squeezed her eyes shut. "I have no idea what's going on with you, but this is so freaking important. This should have been the very *first* thing you showed me, Anna Carmen."

Cici slammed her fists against her twill couch cushion.

After a long moment Cici lifted her head and picked up her phone from where she'd dropped it on the floor.

Cici found Sam's number and pressed "Call."

"What?" he said, his voice groggy with sleep.

"I woke you," Cici said, her voice flat and much too raspy.

"Well, yeah. It's after midnight. What's up?"

Cici heard the sheets shift, the low murmur of a woman's voice.

"Never mind. I didn't realize it was so late. I'm sorry for waking you and Jeannette. Go back to bed. We can talk tomorrow."

Cici pressed "End" and leaned her head back against the couch. She should have known Sam wouldn't let her end the conversation there.

"Why'd you hang up? What did you want?" he said in lieu of a greeting.

Cici sighed into the phone. "I'm really sorry I disturbed you. It can totally wait."

"Your voice is still weird. What's bothering you, Cee?"

She sucked in a breath, trying to calm herself. But that was impossible. The sharpness of the vision, having her twin's thoughts running through her head...

"You need to question Justin Espinoza."

"What? Whoa. Your boyfriend Justin?"

"First off, we're not anything—and thank God for that. Especially after you hear what I have to tell you. Second, Jaycee said she saw him coming out of Miguel's house yesterday. Before we got the call."

That must have been what triggered the dream.

Really, Aci? You're the dead, omniscient one. Do better with directing my subconscious.

"We were at the station. *He* was at the station."

"And you received a call a good hour or more after the EMTs administered Narcan to Miguel. That's plenty of time to get back to the police HQ."

Sam cursed.

"There's more." Because now that she'd had time to think on it, that cold brush on her skin had to have been Anna Carmen trying to warn her.

Sorry, Anna Carmen, for screaming at you the other night. For being mad at you just now.

Cici swallowed. How to explain this to Sam? As close as Sam had been to her sister, they didn't share the immutable bond Cici and Anna Carmen did.

Better to leave that link alone. For now. Focus on the facts. Those were verifiable.

"You also need to ask Justin about why he never told anyone he spoke to Anna Carmen on that pilgrimage to Chimayó."

19

Be great in act, as you have been in thought.
— Shakespeare

Before the clock ticked over to 7:00 a.m., Cici sat next to Rodolfo in the veterinary surgeon's office. Her normally gregarious dog couldn't raise his head but his tail thumped weakly when she crouched down in front of him. His entire chest was shaved, and staring at the vulnerable pink-and-black speckled flesh made her want to weep with frustration.

Killing to protect family, maybe Cici could understand that. Maybe. But shooting a dog in the chest—mere inches from his beautiful, loving heart. *No.* That, there, was cruel.

Cici spent a good hour there, simply petting his great head as the dog labored through each breath.

"Don't die, precious. Please, Rodolfo. Fight for me. I'll bring Mona in to see you again tomorrow."

"I heard that, Rev," Shannon said, coming around the corner.

"You heard nothing," Cici said.

The young woman nodded. She scooted closer and leaned in to Cici's ear. "I'll let you in at seven again."

Cici smiled her thanks at the young woman and continued to stroke Rodolfo's muzzle. The fur there was much shorter, and

Cici could feel each of his bones. Her eyes stung with the tears she tried to battle back.

"And we can get you a girlfriend as soon as you're up and ready to move again. If you want one, that is."

Shannon chuckled as she headed back out to the front, probably to turn on the computers and get the office ready for its daily dose of organized chaos.

Rodolfo whined softly and tried to lick her hand but ended up grimacing in pain when he moved. His breathing labored and he closed his eyes. Cici continued to stroke his head, wishing once again, that she'd made a different choice, been more involved in her sister's life.

Because this? This was the direct result of her lack of attention. Cici leaned in closer still to the dog. She touched her forehead to his. He made a small noise and closed his eyes.

"I have to go to the police station, Rodolfo," Cici whispered. "I'm afraid...I'm afraid Justin might have killed my sister."

———

Sam and Cici sat at one of the conference tables in the main part of the precinct. Justin stared at them from the other side of the table. His hands shook even though they were linked together, resting on the battered oak top. Sam told Cici he refused to pull Justin into an interrogation room.

"He works here, Cee. I can't do that to him." Sam paused, considering. "And you can't come with me."

"I have to," Cici said.

Sam shook his head. "You can't. It's against protocol."

A driving need made Cici grasp Sam's wrist. "I have to," Cici said again, all the emotions from Anna Carmen overflowing in those words. "He knows things. I know he does."

Sam's eyes widened with each word. His mouth gaped as he stared at her. Cici let go of him and stepped back, her breathing still choppy.

"For a moment there, you…you sounded like Anna Carmen. Did that same thing with your mouth she did when she was upset…" Sam shook his head again, as if trying to clear it. "This is weird."

"Please, Sam."

He studied her for a long moment. His eyes seemed both present and calculating. Finally, he said, "I have to make sure it's okay with my boss."

Cici agreed. She waited while Sam spoke to his boss. The man signed off on Sam's request but told Cici she better not get him in trouble.

"I won't," she promised.

He ruminated for another long moment, his pale eyes barely visible under his bushy, white brows. "Fine. But I mean it. Don't screw this up."

Cici wasn't sure if he meant the case, the interview, or something more basic like the conference room. She didn't ask.

She had questions—questions that scared her, especially the more she considered the dream from last night.

For now, though, she sat in her padded chair across the table from Justin, Sam inches away.

Cici still didn't feel safe.

"I never told you, either of you, I spoke to her because it's not like I could bring Anna Carmen back," Justin grumbled. He stared at Cici and Sam across the metal table, his eyes filled with heat.

Cici clasped her hands together on the table, hoping to warm her stiff fingers.

"We know you talked to her that day because I've already spoken with the people who were there," Sam said, his voice carefully modulated.

This must be his detective voice—the one he used with suspects. Cici sucked in a breath, trying to regulate her heartbeat. Being here, questioning Justin…this was surreal. And she'd put this set of events into motion.

Her stomach ached. She didn't want to do this. She didn't want this scenario her mind kept looping through—the scene at the Santuario—to be true.

"You not telling us then…this looks bad, Justin," Sam continued.

Justin's gaze lingered on Cici's red and scabbed hands.

"What happened to you? I never got to ask you yesterday."

"I got in a fight with a chain-link fence," Cici said.

"Looks like you lost," Justin muttered. His eyes flashed up to hers. "You all right?"

"She's fine. Focus on that day in Chimayó. You might have seen her killer," Sam persisted, his voice beginning to grate from the strain of holding on to his temper.

"But I didn't. I'd been through the academy, Sam. I knew what to look for. I was with some of the people from our church. I went over to say hi because Anna Carmen looked so lost in thought. I asked her to join our group. She declined."

"We'll follow up with the list you gave us to make sure," Sam said.

Justin dipped his head, but his eyes narrowed. "Smart."

"Tell me about your uncle Ernesto."

Justin reared back as though Sam had punched him. After a long moment of harsh breathing, he returned his gaze to Sam's.

"*This* is why I didn't say anything. Ernesto was a lowlife, drug-selling piece of scum. He killed people to protect his drug trafficking."

Justin's gaze skittered to Cici's before landing back on Sam's. She sat up straighter, knowing he didn't want her in the room—yet hoping he would be compelled to tell the truth because she was there.

The silence in the room fell heavy, accusatory, around all three of them. Sam reached forward and wrapped his long fingers around the Styrofoam cup in front of him.

Sam took a sip, eyes still trained on Justin. He set the cup back on the metal table and straightened the notes in front of him.

"Tell us why you were at Miguel Sanchez's the day he ended up in the back of an ambulance."

Justin's eyebrows rose to his hairline. He whistled.

"No wonder I'm in here," Justin mused. "You really think I had something to do with this, don't you?"

Sam leaned forward, eyes narrowing. "I'm asking the questions, here, Justin."

"Wow," Justin whispered. "You do."

Silence. The two men studied each other, causing Cici to shift in her chair.

"I don't know what to think, Justin," she said, the compulsion to speak too strong to ignore. "But I'm scared." She took a deep breath. "Please tell us what happened at the Sanchez's house. Please."

"I was…following a lead," Justin said, his cheeks turning a ruddy shade.

"A lead? On what?"

Justin's face turned redder. "I know I'm not an investigator, but I heard something…and I wanted to see if it panned out."

"What was this lead?" Sam asked, his voice flinty.

Justin hung his head. "It's connected. To Ernesto."

"Who's dead?" Sam asked.

"That's the official line from Mexico," Justin returned.

"Are you saying you don't believe it?"

"I'm saying…I'm not sure I want to tell you what I suspected."

Sam leaned forward. Cici saw how tight his hands were fisted in his lap. She hadn't seen Sam this angry since…well, since Anna Carmen's funeral.

"We have two accounts now that you were on Juan's street yesterday," Sam said. "Thanks to your own written statement that you handed over twenty minutes ago, we know you spoke with Anna Carmen within minutes of her death. You have been my friend for over twenty years, Justin, but right now, I'm starting to believe you've not only lied to me, you're an accessory to Anna Carmen's murder."

"Whatever you tell me now won't bring Anna Carmen back," Cici said, leaning forward and wrapping both of her hands around Justin's larger one. "Please, Justin. For her. Please."

Justin pulled his hand out from between hers and patted them both. His hand was warm, comforting. Cici began to relax.

"I told you it was a *potential* lead. I parked across the street."

"In front of Miguel Sanchez's house," Sam said, still frowning.

"Yeah." Justin blew out a breath. "I never got out of my car. I did, however, take a bunch of pictures on my camera."

"Of what?" Sam asked.

"Susan Johnson."

"Why?"

Justin rolled his lips into his mouth.

"The potential lead," Sam prompted. "Did it pan out?"

"I don't think so."

"Why's that?"

"Because someone tried to kill Cici's dog with an arrow."

"Tried to shoot me first," Cici muttered.

Justin sat up straighter. "What?"

"Mind if we look?" Sam asked.

"At what?" Justin asked, still staring at Cici.

"The photos you took," Sam said, exasperation creeping into his voice.

Justin shook his head. "I was going to give them to you anyway."

Cici eyes filled with tears and her nose plugged. "I'm sorry, Justin."

He turned toward her—the same caring eyes she'd seen in her kitchen last week. Her chest ached. Justin helped Sam find her on the Dale Ball Trails. He helped get Rodolfo to the vet's vehicle.

"What's got you so worked up, Cee?" Sam asked.

"What was going on with you and Anna Carmen?" Cici asked. "Evan said he saw you with her the night before she died."

No, that wasn't true. Evan said Anna Carmen spent time with Donald Johnson. But as soon as the words left Cici's lips, she knew them to be true.

Sure, Cici was angry with her sister, but she also trusted Anna Carmen with her life. Just as Anna Carmen trusted Cici with her story. Even when it wasn't the pretty one Anna Carmen wanted it to be. That's why she showed Cici that conversation in the dream.

Cici concentrated, pulling back up the emotion from her vision last night. Dread. Anna Carmen hadn't wanted to see Justin, hadn't wanted to talk to him.

"Nothing," he said.

"Justin, I'm going to tell you right now that I know you're lying," Cici said.

His gaze caught hers as his mouth turned down.

"How do you know that?" Sam demanded.

"I just do," Cici said, her voice brooking no argument. "What happened between you and Anna Carmen that made Evan so upset?"

Justin held her gaze so long Cici had to blink.

"Ask him."

Cici looked down at the table, sifting through the images and emotions she'd experienced last night. Nothing. Cici had nothing further.

She raised her gaze and saw something dark flash in Justin's eyes. That soft, subtle breeze touched Cici's cheek, her lips.

"How long had you been in love with her?" Cici asked, her voice quiet.

Justin's lips slammed together tighter. Sam straightened in his chair.

"You did. You loved her," Cici said.

The certainty grew. Cici could feel her sister there, next to her, feel her agitation and excitement as Cici homed in on this truth. What had Anna Carmen said? That Cici had to fix what Anna Carmen broke. But it wasn't Anna Carmen who tried to destroy her relationship with Evan.

"And you told…" Cici wanted to look over. See her sister. She kept her eyes on Justin's face by sheer strength of will. "You told Evan *you* wanted Anna Carmen."

"I think I might need a lawyer," Justin said. "Definitely *not* Evan."

"Justin." Cici's voice was soft, pleading. "My sister's dead, and this is the first real lead the police have. You loved her. I *need* you to tell us what happened."

Justin's eyes turned to ice and his face settled into immutable lines. "I don't need to tell you a damn thing about my private life. Either of you. And Evan's a lying piece of human refuse who can go screw himself."

Justin crossed his arms over his chest and glared.

Sam stood, his metal chair grating on the linoleum, causing Cici to jump. Sam touched her shoulder, made a gesture for her to stand. She did, on shaky legs.

Sam took her arm and led her from the room.

Cici stepped out of the room and leaned back against the

wall, trying to stem her shaking.

"Did that go as badly as I think it did?" she asked.

"Worse," Sam said. He reread the note Cici had given him. "Why didn't you tell me what you suspected?"

This time, Cici's face brightened and she dropped her gaze to her sneaker-clad feet. "I didn't want it to be about Justin."

"And now? What do you think now, Cee?"

She swallowed hard. After taking one deep breath, then a second, Cici faced Sam directly. "I think he's lied to all of us. About all of this."

Sam stuttered forward, sadness darkening his eyes. "Ah, Cee. I hate this. For both of us."

Cici rested her head against his shoulder and drew a shuddering breath. "So do I," she managed to choke out around the knot of emotion snarled in her throat. Sam patted her back, his large hand soothing.

Jen, one of the receptionists, rounded the corner and paused in front of Sam, her uncertain gaze darting back and forth between them. "Detective? You've got a call you're going to want to take."

"All right. You know who it is?"

Jen shrugged. "Not real sure. Probably something you should…ah…go see to."

Sam sucked his lower lip into his mouth. "Can you tell whomever it is I'll have to call them back? I need to speak with the captain."

Jen's eye darted toward the closed conference door, and Cici's heart sank. Justin's past—especially where it entwined with her sister's—might be murky, but…Cici didn't believe, could not believe, Justin had killed Anna Carmen.

Not after that first dream where Anna Carmen very clearly did not know who stabbed her.

"Erm, I think you're going to want to take the call," Jen said. "It's important."

Was that why her sister showed her those visions in that order? Cici grasped Justin's part in the drama might prove larger than she would've imagined, but he wasn't the one who did the deed and took Anna Carmen's life.

She didn't think.

She leaned her head back against the wall and shut her eyes. She was tired. Soul-consuming tired, as she'd been after Anna Carmen's death.

"What if I sit with Justin while you take your call?" Cici suggested.

Sam shoved the corner of his thumb into his mouth—a sure sign of agitation. He only ever bit his cuticles under duress.

"It'll be okay," Cici said, keeping her voice low.

"How do you know that? I lost Anna Carmen." Sam turned his anguished eyes to her. He took in her every feature in a way that warmed her heart. "I can't lose you, too, Cee. I *can't*." His voice broke.

"I'll wait right here with her, Detective," Jen offered.

"That'll work fine," Cici said with a bit of a smile, trying to find her equilibrium after being the recipient of Sam's hungry gaze.

"I'll be right back," Sam said.

"All right."

Cici watched Sam hurry down the hall toward his desk. She sighed, her shoulders slumping with fatigue as she stared at the door.

"Hard part of the legal system," Jen said.

"What's that?" Cici asked.

"Doing what's right. That's the hardest part sometimes. Especially in a town this size. You know the people brought in. Think you *know* them. But sometimes they have such deep-seated secrets you find they're strangers."

"Yeah," Cici said, blowing out a breath. "Yeah." She stood up. "You know—you gave me an idea. Mind if I call someone?"

"Sure." Jen leaned against the white, scuffed wall where Cici had rested moments before. She stared down the corridor toward the bull pen that housed the officers' desks, away from Cici. Cici would need to thank Jen for giving her as much privacy as she could.

———

Cici stepped away a few paces and thumbed through her phone to find Evan's number. The hall was quiet—probably because Justin was the only one in one of these rooms right now.

She held her breath as it dialed.

"What do you want?" he growled.

Evan's greeting was as caustic as the last interaction they'd had. How had she missed his pain?

"You know Anna Carmen never had a relationship with Justin."

"Oh. Really? And how do you know that?" His voice sharpened.

"Evan. She was my *identical twin*. We talked about your wedding, how many kids you'd have and what you'd name them. She was conflicted about leaving her students at Capitol, but she planned to do it because it meant she'd get to be with *you*."

Cici chuckled but the sound was dry as the snow that blew away faster than a tumbleweed.

"She loved you despite your profession," Cici murmured. "You have *no idea* how hard that must have been for her because our dad is a massive dick."

Silence filled the space between them. Finally, Evan sighed. Cici's stomach dipped even as hope began to burn in her chest.

"I heard your words, but they don't compute. Something about you being a person of god and saying 'massive dick' screams wrong."

For the first time since coming home, Evan's voice lost some of its frostiness.

"She considered you her soul mate," Cici went on, needing to get this out.

Evan's breath broke and his voice caught when he said, "Are you…really?"

Cici remembered the dream, her sister's eyes when she'd asked about courage. "I'm sure."

"Jesus, Cee. I mean…sorry about the Lord's name. Wow. Wow. That's…wow."

"Why didn't you take the job in Scottsdale?" Cici asked.

"It fell through," Evan replied. "I was told I'd been blackballed from any of the big firms."

Cici's brows knit tight. "Why?"

"This was the day Anna Carmen died. Before. I wanted to talk to her about it. I called her."

"I know." Cici didn't mention she knew because she'd dreamed it. She didn't think Evan would appreciate her being privy to that much personal information.

"What happened, Evan? I need to understand."

"You're sure?" He asked, his voice cracking. "I was the one she considered her soul mate?"

Anna Carmen's eyes in the white bird's face flashed into Cici's mind again. The sheer emotion in Anna Carmen's eyes caused Cici's to water. She sniffled.

"I'm one hundred percent positive. I thought it was so strange when you mentioned Aci met with Donald—like you thought there could be something there when you were all she saw, all she wanted."

Again, Evan had to swallow. Cici understood how that ball of emotion ripped into the throat.

"The firm was Gladstone and Associates." Evan's voice was hoarse.

Cici couldn't breathe. How hadn't she known that? In all their conversations, Anna Carmen never said what firm Evan planned to work for...and now she knew why. Because Evan planned to work for their father's former lover, KaraLynn.

"I'd been offered a pretty great deal there and I'd accepted it, in writing. They had to pay me the signing bonus after they rescinded the offer."

"That's KaraLynn's personal team."

"Yeah. KaraLynn Gladstone."

"KaraLynn as in my *almost*-step mom. She and my dad split earlier this year. Amicably, which means she was seeing someone else and he caught her, I'd bet." Cici swallowed. "That kind of money and power is never split amicably."

"I work in tax law. I never understood why they wouldn't want me there."

"I don't think it had anything to do with you. I think KaraLynn and my father knew about one of Donald's clients."

"Who?"

"Ernesto Espinoza."

Evan's breath fractured into the phone. "The drug trafficker?"

"Yeah. That guy. Donald Johnson represented some of his interests. At least according to Susan."

"Shit. Damn. Shit. Sorry, Cee. How didn't I know that?" Evan muttered.

"It was all hushed," Cici said. "That's what money does. It buys silence. And compliance."

"You think…you think Anna Carmen talked to Donald and then…then…because of the drug lord…she's dead," Evan said.

Evan sniffled. This was the man Anna Carmen had loved— the one who could finally mourn her and, when he was ready, move on. Cici's eyes began to fill with tears at the thought of Evan finding someone to spend his life with. That's part of what her sister wanted—her great love to be happy.

Oh, Aci, I don't know if I'd have that grace in me.

"I thought she was seeing Justin Espinoza," he said. "She'd been spending time with him and Donald. She wouldn't tell me why. Cici, if you're right, then you have to bring in Justin. He's an accessory to Anna Carmen's murder."

Cici blew out a breath. "Sam's questioning him now. Back then…when Anna Carmen died…wasn't Justin a new police recruit then?"

"Yes, fresh out of the academy. Why?"

"I'm not sure. Just something about the timing seems important."

Evan cleared his throat. Cici heard a tapping. Maybe a pen on his desk.

"She got in Justin's car the night before she went to the pilgrimage," Evan said. "I stopped by her work, wanted to see if she was okay about Marco's death…I saw him kiss her."

"You were there?" Cici asked, gripping the phone tighter. "Who else did you see?"

Evan made a frustrated sound. "I don't know. I'll have to think about it."

"Do. And call me," Cici said.

"You really don't think she was having an affair with Justin?" Evan asked again.

Anna Carmen's regret when she thought of Evan in her last moments made more sense. By playing a secretive game, Anna Carmen got herself killed and broke her lover's heart.

"You were her *every* thought, Evan. At least all the good ones."

Evan hung up after promising again to call if he thought of anything else. Cici walked back down the hall, past the officer toward Sam's desk.

Sam was still on the phone, so Cici nodded to Jen.

"Can you find me Officer Loomis?" Cici asked.

"Sure," Jen said. She trotted back to her desk and made a couple of calls.

Cici headed back to the corridor with the conference rooms. She waited for Kevin outside the door, peeking in to see Justin slumped at the table.

"Will you come in here?" Cici asked Kevin once he got close enough to where she stood. "I'd like to have another person in the room while I talk to Justin."

"Okay," Kevin said.

Cici smiled a little. She'd known his curiosity would get the better of him. A police employee brought in for questioning in an ongoing investigation would be the talk of the precinct for months, maybe years.

"This is over the top, you know," Justin said on a sigh. "I didn't hurt Anna Carmen."

"I need to apologize to you," Cici said.

Officer Loomis strolled over behind her chair. Cici patted the chair next to her, but he remained a tall, silent presence behind her.

Justin blinked rapidly, clearly surprised by this turn of events. "Thanks, I guess."

She watched Justin for a long moment, taking special care to focus on the eyes he refused to keep trained on her face.

"I honestly didn't think you had it in you to call my father."

He jerked as though he'd been struck, his skin paling below his tan.

"What do you mean?" Justin croaked.

"Frank Gurule enjoyed blackballing his future son-in-law, I'm sure. That's what he gets off on most—power. And since the pedigree of the law firm here in Santa Fe wasn't as perfect as Evan believed it to be, that leaves me curious."

Cici leaned forward, her hands splayed flat on the cool wood table. The outlines of the abrasions on her hands stood out starkly on her normally pale skin. At least this way her hands appeared steady. Like she was in control.

"About two things. First, how did you know Donald Johnson represented Ernesto Espinoza?"

Justin paled further. "I'm not answering that."

Cici cocked her head as Justin shifted in his seat.

"All right," Cici said, her voice neutral as if they were discussing the weather—not the decisions that led to her twin's murder. "I'm sure Susan or even one of the clerks at the office will find that information eventually. The other piece I don't understand is what, exactly, my father promised you in exchange for helping him destroy Anna Carmen's happiness."

Silence. Justin didn't move. Kevin Loomis shifted behind her, clearly uncomfortable with this line of questioning. Cici waited.

Justin raised his gaze for a second and Cici smiled with gentle assurance.

"Because that's what he did, you know. With your help." She leaned in, closer. "Frank Gurule destroyed Anna Carmen. Might as well have stabbed his own child in the back."

Again, she waited. Justin swallowed hard enough for his Adam's apple to bob deeply.

"I hope what you got out of the deal was better than Anna Carmen's reward," Cici said.

Justin mumbled toward the table.

"What was that?" Cici asked.

"He got me a place on the police force," Justin muttered.

"How?" Cici asked.

Justin's face contorted with fury. "Because I should have failed one of my classes, okay? School was never easy for me."

"Investigation," Cici murmured. "You said you were bad at investigation. But you found out something…about Ernesto. Or was it about Donald? Is that why you brought him in to meet Anna Carmen?"

He stared at her, his eyes haunted but his lips compressed tightly.

"She's dead. I can't bring her back," Cici said, her voice soft. "But telling me can help me save lives."

Justin crossed his arms over his chest. "And cost me mine. I'm willing to do a lot for you, Cee. I've told you things that'll probably land me in jail. I…" He blew out a breath and pain etched across his face. "I deserve that. But I'm not willing to die for you."

"Not even now that we know your lack of testimony might well be the reason my sister, the woman you profess to have loved since high school, is dead?"

"Your sister died because she insisted on sticking her nose into a drug lord's business!" Justin shot back. "She signed her death warrant as soon as she took the first picture. She and that Sanchez boy."

20

The tempter or the tempted, who sins most?
— Shakespeare

Cici froze. Juan's older brother who was found in a bathroom, face blue, eyes open. She'd asked Sam for the details.

Now, she wished she hadn't.

"What picture?"

Justin sighed, closing his eyes. When he opened them, they were bloodshot. Grief ravaged his face, causing him to look ten, maybe fifteen years older.

"God. I shouldn't have said that." He shook his head, his lips trembling.

"What happened to the pictures Anna Carmen took, Justin? And just how deep into this investigation have you been?"

Justin dropped his eyes back to the table where his hands were clasped loosely together. "Enough to know saying another word is going to cost me my life."

Sam yanked open the door to the room, his face a milky mask against his too-dark eyes.

"Let's go," he said, scowling.

Cici winced when Sam caught her hand and tugged her from the chair. His sense of urgency pounded against her skin, the heat of it causing Cici's heart rate to rage in her chest.

"Sorry," he murmured, softening his grip. "Forgot about the cuts. Hurry."

"Oh, no," Cici groaned, her worst nightmare coming true. "Who's dead now?"

Sam's scowl built darker. "No one's dead. We found Susan Johnson. She's at her house. She wants to talk to you."

"What about Justin?" Cici asked, jogging to keep up with Sam's larger strides.

"Officer Loomis will keep an eye on him until his shift ends. I asked my boss to assign someone else. It'll probably be Damian. He's on probation and gets all the shit assignments right now."

"What did Damian do?" Cici shook her head. "Never mind. More pressing matter: Aren't Justin and Damian related?"

"We live in a town of less than a hundred thousand people," Sam said, exasperation building in his voice. "That's been around for over four-hundred years. Most of us who've been here for any length of time are related or at least know each other well."

"But—"

"Damian will do his job," Sam snapped. "He has to, and the chief is involved now because this whole situation with Justin makes his department look bad."

"Especially when it comes out who helped Justin get his job with the police department," Cici murmured.

"I heard that," Sam said. "You make one helluva good detective, by the way."

"I don't want to be one," Cici responded.

Sam stopped at the doors and turned back to look at her. His eyes remained stormy and his mouth pulled down in frustration and concern. "Yeah. I get that."

———

"How'd you find Susan?" Cici asked as she climbed into the white, American-made sedan. At least this vehicle had been parked in the large parking garage, so entering the car didn't lead to immediate and near asphyxiation.

Only people who didn't live here considered Santa Fe summers a joke—but when the city was in the middle of a heat wave (as it was now), the temperatures were on par with Phoenix and just as nasty.

"She came home about an hour ago. I spoke with her on the phone, and she asked to speak to you, specifically."

Sam, whose second career should be NASCAR driving, pulled up in front of the large, stately home a few minutes later. Cici exited the vehicle, hand to stomach, feeling ill and not just because of Sam's driving.

She tottered up the steps to the Johnsons' large, beaten-wood front door. She knocked.

No one answered.

Cici knocked again.

The door swung open a little, giving them a glimpse into the opulent rotunda-style entry. Small tumbled-marble and glass tiles decorated the floor in a variety of murals, each centered around the Zia, the New Mexican symbol of the sun.

Sam pushed the door open farther, his gaze cautious as he kept Cici behind him. After another moment, he sighed and plucked his phone from his pocket. He spoke into it slowly, carefully, to describe exactly what was happening.

A loud, low "poof" ripped through the house, slamming into Cici's ears. Another low, dead thud. Then another and another, followed by tinkling glass.

Sam shoved Cici back onto the porch, where she tripped over a potted plant and landed on her hands and knees. Pain lanced through her right elbow as it took the brunt of her weight. Almost immediately, more pain shot through her left knee where she caught some rough material, ripping her skin.

"Shots fired. Repeat shots fired. Address 392…"

Sam disappeared into the house, pistol drawn, phone shoved into his pocket.

Cici rolled away from the door, unsure if Sam or whomever fired the weapon—at least she assumed the sounds she'd heard were a gun—ran out the front.

She leaned against the side of the rough stucco wall for a long moment, trying to quiet her pounding heart and ease the rush of blood through her ears. After a few shaky breaths, Cici stood, using the wall for support. She winced at the cut on her knee but tottered toward the door.

"Cici!" Sam called.

"Yeah?"

"Come here! Office. Follow my voice. Now."

Cici hurried forward. Susan lay on the floor, blood seeping through her white silk blouse, the loose bow tie around her high collar completely undone and now crimson.

Cici sank to her knees, uncaring about her own small injury.

Sam leaned over the older woman, applying pressure to the

wound, his face chalky, his eyes too large and haunted.

"Is she okay?" Cici whispered.

"No," Sam said.

"Cee," Susan panted. "Cee. Need to tell you…some things. Donnie had…" Her breath rattled wet, thick, became more labored. "A safe. Back of his closet. Another at the office. He was…" She paused her face paling as her eyes darkened.

"Shh. It's okay. You can tell me more once the paramedics help you," Cici said, her voice catching.

"No." Susan's voice was strident, angry. "No time. 'S how I found out about all this. Went through the safe here."

Her breath grew thicker, like a barge that's sucked up the incorrect mixture of liquid and air. Cici gripped Susan's chilled hand as she tried to swallow down the panic bubbling over.

"They followed me. I want it to end."

"What needs to end?" Sam asked.

Sam adjusted his grip on the towel he'd found. Cici swallowed as she watched the red seep against the light blue.

Susan tried to lift her body up to see him but gave up quickly. Sam placed a gentle hand on her shoulder.

"Easy," he said. "Hold tight. I called an ambulance."

"The threats. The fear."

Susan choked, tried to cough. A thin trickle of pink-tinged saliva slid past her lips.

"Donnie worked…with the DEA. After Anna Carmen's death…he wanted to fix it."

"Why now?" Cici asked.

"They…"

Susan struggled, her chest unable to expand. Her face contorted.

"Stopped. Had a baby. Moved. Donnie kept an ear out. Passed along what he could."

"I thought he was taking opioids, using the post office in Madrid to funnel those meds."

"He did," Susan rasped. "That's how it started. Drugs, blackmail."

Her lips tinged blue. This time, more blood dribbled across her lips.

"Ernesto wanted…trade. His expertise…not implicated…not killed."

Susan closed her eyes. Cici gripped her hand, thinking of her father, KaraLynn.

"When you're considered one of the city's elite, your reputation matters," she murmured.

"True. But Donnie…he tried to talk Anna Carmen into… dropping the questions. She…wouldn't. Not once Rosalia…was murdered."

"Why was she?" Sam asked.

"Rosalia was…friends…with Ernesto's…wife. Her hairdresser…knew…their plans…wanted a…cut of money."

Cici blew out a breath. Greed and power. Two of the oldest— and ugliest motivators in human history.

"Why didn't Anna Carmen go to the police?" Cici asked, the anger she'd felt at her sister building inside her again.

"She…did."

Cici froze. Slowly, she raised her eyes to Sam, who shook his head slowly, mouth set to a thin slash.

"SFPD has no record," Sam said.

"She *did*," Susan insisted. "Donnie…worried…about that."

"Enough to tell Ernesto?" Sam asked, his voice flat and cynical.

Susan's eyes dimmed. Her lips and cheeks lost color so she looked more like a waxy model than an actual person.

"Yes."

"But…" Cici shook her head. "Why work so hard to get me to come back here? To donate to the church?"

Cici recoiled as the thought slithered through her. No. No, she didn't want blood money.

Susan tried to squeeze her fingers, but she didn't have the strength.

"A type of restitution," Susan rasped. "Anna Carmen…feel badly over that."

"You helped finance our building. My salary," Cici yelped, her nose burning with tears as she remembered her dream from last night.

The pain and fear her sister felt as she was stabbed and after, as she died—that she transferred to Cici in the dream, kept haunting her now.

"When Anna Carmen died," Sam said, "did you know Ernesto killed her?"

"Don't think he did. Postal inspectors…stopped drug ring then…but…murders…personal. Donnie's death …personal."

"Who killed him?" Cici demanded. "Why?"

Susan's lips quirked up briefly. "Not me."

"You knew. When you came to my office, you *knew* all this."

"No. Thought I'd be okay…he never shared…documents with me. I was wrong."

"Did you see the person, Susan?" Sam asked. "The one who shot you."

"No. Just…big black truck…parked in back."

Cici fisted her hands.

"The wife," Cici muttered. "Ernesto's wife. Maybe she's the one who called in Donald's death. The perfume you smelled."

"Check the safes," Susan coughed out. "I didn't have…time to get to…the one at the office…"

Susan closed her eyes.

She was dead by the time the paramedics arrived three minutes later.

———

"Think she was telling the truth this time?" Cici asked.

"Death bed confessions tend to be truthful," Sam replied.

"But Anna Carmen talking to the police?"

Cici looked up as Sam watched the team bag Susan's body for the medical investigator.

She rubbed her palms up her arms, trying to warm herself, but her insides—her heart—remained frigid. She might never thaw again. Her sister was dead even after she did the right thing—went to the police as she'd been taught.

Her twin was still *dead*.

And Cici had to move on. Had to find the killer. Rodolfo deserved it, as did her sister, Marco Sanchez, and Susan.

Cici raised her hand and pressed it to her mouth. She closed her eyes and drew in a long, deep, steadying breath. She tried again, then again. Many breaths later, she faced Sam, who'd waited patiently for her to pull herself back together.

"So, you think Donald was working with the DEA to bring down the drug ring?"

"Makes sense." Sam slid his hands into his pockets. "More sense than most of what we've heard. Especially if the post office inspectors did shut down the last round."

"Can you check on that?" Cici asked. "I never heard about a postal bust."

"Neither did I," Sam said, his eyes narrowed. "Doesn't mean it didn't happen, just that it was silenced. The only reason to silence a big bust is if you're going after a *bigger* player."

"Donald was in Madrid once a week," Cici said slowly. "That's what Jaycee said. And Jeannette said he visited the Mayor's office."

Sam nodded, approval lighting his eye.

"I'll talk to Jeannette in just a minute, but my guess is that Donald Johnson met someone there—in the mayor's office," Sam said. "An informant or officer. Probably DEA. Maybe Jeannette knows who that is."

"What? Why would she?"

"Because the DEA handles most of the drug cases in the country."

"Their investigation supersedes yours?" Cici asked.

She shivered again. She hated the idea of her church being funded off blood money.

Sam laid his hand on the back of her neck, sliding his large palm under her hair. After another few minutes, her shivering eased. She wanted to say thanks, but Sam was staring off in the distance, working over the problem in his mind.

"I wouldn't say that," Sam said. "More like we're both on the same big team. Good, the forensics team is here."

"Really?" Cici asked. "I thought the federal investigation always won out. Isn't that true?"

"You ready to go?" Sam asked, ignoring her last question. "Forensics will take awhile, and I need to get my evidence together to request some warrants."

"Um. Sure," Cici mumbled.

"Nothing like being enthusiastic there, my girl."

———

Sam drove to the police station where he spent the next hour and a half on the phone or in and out of his superior's office while Cici cooled her heels in the tucked-away corner Sam called an office.

When he returned the next time, his face was animated.

"Got our warrant," he said. "Call Evan. See if he'll meet you at the law offices."

"Why?"

Sam pulled her to her feet and shepherded her from the office.

"Do you need to check on Justin?" Cici asked.

"Did. He's in another room, being watched."

"Oh." Cici hustled after Sam, who used his long legs to their great advantage, impatient to get to his car.

"I don't understand why I need to call Evan," Cici said as she slid into the car. "What are you worried about?"

He turned to look at Cici, his eyes dark. "What am I not

worried about? We have two more people dead in the last two weeks, one hell of a drug trafficking story going and a whole lot of people who could be complicit, colluding, or completely unaware. I'm hoping for option three, but from what you told me about J.R., I'm concerned he's in the former camp."

"Complicit or colluding?" Cici asked, nervous flutters building in her stomach.

"Right. Which is why I'd like to get into Donald's office without J.R. knowing."

"How are you going to get in the safe?" Cici asked.

They stopped at another light. Sam turned to look at her again. "You're assuming the safe is still in his office."

Cici couldn't think of a response, so she pulled out her phone and called Evan.

"Cee, I'm not ready for another round," he said on a sigh.

"I need your help," Cici wheedled. "It's important."

"Related to Anna Carmen's death?" he asked.

Cici paused, considering. Sam hadn't said she couldn't tell Evan, but, then again, Sam suspected J.R.

"Yes. Please?" Cici said.

"All right," Evan grumbled. "But you owe me details."

"Beer and hot wings still your thing? We can talk over those."

"It's annoying that your sister told you everything," Evan said. But a hint of laughter seeped into his tone.

Cici smiled but it was softer than most. She liked this part of her new knowledge Anna Carmen imparted. "Yeah, but that's how I know how much she loved you. Your office. Soon as you can."

Evan choked up a little and had to clear his throat. "I'll meet you there," Evan said before hanging up.

Sam raised his eyebrows in question.

"I'm guessing about twenty minutes," Cici replied.

"Cool. I could use a bite. How about the food truck on the corner of Old Santa Fe Trail?"

"Sure." Cici wasn't hungry, but she should probably try to eat something. She shoved her phone back into her pocket. Now seemed as good a time to ask as any. "How'd you manage with Anna Carmen dating Evan? I mean, they were serious."

Sam faced the windshield in front of him but Cici caught him lowering his eyes as he shrugged.

"You know how your sister was," Sam said. "She made time to hang out. Sometimes Evan came, too."

"I didn't know that," Cici murmured.

"This was before I went to Denver for the task force," Sam said.

"You miss it?" Cici asked.

Sam sat, quiet. "Sometimes. You miss Boston?"

"Yeah. But I came back here with a purpose. One I intend to fulfill."

The silence settled back around them.

"You know she planned to marry him?" Cici asked.

They'd never discussed Anna Carmen's love life before, but Cici always assumed Sam wouldn't marry—or even date all that seriously—because Anna Carmen chose another man.

She wondered what it would be like to pine for someone she'd never have. She did, a little, when she thought of how she could be in South America right now, covered in mosquito bites and pregnant with her first child. If she hadn't broken up with

Lyndon—and if they'd been a better fit.

"I was happy for her," Sam said. "Really happy because she'd found the man she was destined to be with."

Sam's brow wrinkled and he glanced at her from the corner of his eye. Oh, no, she'd hurt him. Cici wanted to reach out and offer comfort but Sam seemed to pull tauter when she lifted her hand. Time to change the subject.

"They still have the bleu cheese green chile burger there?" Cici asked.

"Yep."

She leaned back against the headrest and closed her eyes. "I haven't had one of those in ages."

———

Evan unlocked the door to the office, only a slight scowl tugging at his features when he spotted Sam trailing Cici.

"Should I have asked for a warrant, Detective?"

"You in possession of something you don't want me to see, Counselor?"

But even as he said it, Sam pulled a document from his back pocket. Cici's heart fluttered as he handed the paper to Evan, whose face remained impassive as he examined it and then handed it back.

"Will you two play nice?" Cici said in exasperation. "I want this done. For some reason, I've got a bad feeling."

"Not the words I wanted to hear coming out of your mouth," Sam muttered.

"Why?" Evan asked, pressing the elevator button.

"She has better intuition than anyone I've ever worked with.

She was already at the airport, talking to the ticket agent when news of Anna Carmen came through."

Sam had called the station at her request after lunch to make sure Justin was still being held. He was, so Cici decided to keep her mouth shut. Her intuition wasn't always spot on and Sam could have pointed that out. She appreciated that he didn't.

Evan turned to apprise Cici, who turned red under his heavy gaze. "I didn't know that."

"For as similar as they look, the Gurule ladies have always been vastly different."

Evan turned to study Sam for the rest of the elevator ride. The car opened and Evan stepped forward, holding open the door.

"I'll keep that in mind, Detective," Evan said.

"Glad to hear it, Counselor," Sam replied.

Sam dipped his head in a nod as he stepped out behind Cici.

Evan led them down the hall. He'd just opened his mouth to speak when Sam pulled out his gun and stepped in front of both Evan and Cici. He raised the police-issue pistol, keeping both hands around the finger grips, his pointer finger resting lightly on the trigger.

Get down, he mouthed.

Cici crouched back against the wall, pulling Evan down next to her. He opened his mouth but Cici covered it with her hand and shook her head. Sam stepped forward, silent, so that Cici could hear the faint scuffling of feet and papers. Evan tensed under her fingers but Cici kept her hand there—a silent deterrent.

The door to the office was closed, the name Donald Johnson still embossed in fancy gold paint on the door.

Sam stood to the side of the door, glanced back to make sure Cici and Evan were out of harm's way. Evan hovered next to Cici in a protective gesture she found strange.

Sam slid his left hand forward and inched it onto the door handle. He turned it slowly. In one motion, he shoved open the door and stepped into the doorway, gun leveled.

A long silence ensued. His gun never wavered, but Sam blinked, his shoulders bunching tighter.

Beside her, Evan tensed as if Sam's tension passed to him.

Just when Cici thought she might scream or laugh or do something else equally as dangerous or embarrassing, Sam hissed.

"Jeannette?"

21

Go wisely and slowly. Those who rush stumble and fall. — Shakespeare

The woman's sweet, melodic voice filled the space around them, making Cici's nerve endings quiver.

"Hi, Sam."

Cici's jaw dropped open. She couldn't believe it. Evan pulled Cici to her feet, but Sam glanced back and shook his head.

Cici pressed against the wall again, her heart thundering. Sam didn't think the threat had passed.

Sancte deus. Now they had to worry about *Jeannette?*

"Why are you here?" Sam asked.

"I really think the better question is how you got in here. Do you have a warrant?"

Sam's scowl blackened further. "Why are you packing up those boxes?"

"If you're interested in that, I'll need to see your paperwork, Detective."

"Do *you* have a warrant?" Sam shot back.

"An ongoing one with Judge Rivera."

"Why are you working with a federal judge? What force do you work for, Jeannette? Don't blow smoke up my ass because it's way too late for that."

"Mmm. I've always liked how smart you are, Sam. Want to guess?"

Evan choked again. "Is she always this snarky?" he whispered to Cici.

Cici shrugged. Jeannette had always been kind, quiet—like the voice she'd first spoken in here today. Cici had no idea the pretty blonde led a double life.

"What agency do you work for?" Sam demanded again.

Cici waited for him to lower his weapon. He didn't. She pressed her hands to her roiling stomach.

"DEA," Jeannette said. "I wondered if you'd catch on after I told Cici we saw quite a bit of Donald." She sighed. "I definitely went too far with that statement."

"I'd like to see your credentials," Sam said.

There was another flurry of sound, then Jeannette said, "Satisfied?"

"Hardly," Sam muttered. But he finally lowered his gun. With jerky movements, he replaced it in his holster.

"So, how'd you get in?" Jeannette asked.

"Evan Reynolds."

"Oh? So, he's the one in the hall? I thought I heard three sets of feet. Let me guess, you have the lovely reverend with you, too."

Sam sighed, his face pained as he nodded Evan and Cici over. Cici peeked around the edge of the door to see Jeannette packing up a third file box of papers.

"I assume your clear-out means you don't intend to share those documents with local PD?" Sam asked, hurt and frustration lacing his voice.

"Good assumption, Detective. This is a delicate case we've been working nearly two years to close. It's a huge entity across several states, plus the Mexican border. I can't have local law enforcement screwing it up now."

"Think you're going to nail Ernesto Espinoza?" Sam asked.

Jeannette was good, but she still paused in the transfer of another batch of documents, her entire body tightening.

"Who?" she asked, raising those beautiful blue eyes to Sam's.

"You know his wife's involved," Sam said, leaning against the doorjamb and practically pushing Cici and Evan back out into the hall.

"What?" Jeannette's voice turned biting. Definitely not the sweet blond woman Cici thought she knew.

"Oh, and Susan Johnson's dead."

"When?" Jeannette snapped.

Cici shivered. Jeannette's voice turned colder than ice and twice as sharp.

Sam stepped into the room, keeping his gun by his leg. "Just saying we could help each other."

"This is my case, Chastain," Jeannette snarled. "Back off."

"I'll just call your supervisor. Herman Baca, right? He'll be pretty unhappy when I tell him the task force with the sheriff's department and Española PD didn't get put together because you refused to let it."

Jeannette paused in her packing. Cici didn't understand what Sam was saying, but it was clear Jeannette did.

"Last time Herm and I spoke, he was livid when I mentioned

the problem with my warrant for the post office on Pacheco. I'm assuming he spoke with you about that?"

Sam shifted, so Cici couldn't see Jeannette past his back, but the thud of the box and the curse words were fairly illustrative of Jeannette's deteriorating mood.

"What do you want?" she demanded.

"First, for you to stop trying to hamstring my investigation."

Cici caught the side of Sam's face and his narrowed eye.

"That might be how they do it up in Denver, or even..." He considered Jeannette for a long moment. "The Dallas office."

Jeannette remained quiet this time, but even from her vantage point behind Sam, Cici knew he'd scored some kind of point.

"By the way," Sam said, "I already told Baca I want to see those papers you're so keen to move out."

"How do you know Baca's in charge?" Jeannette asked, exasperated.

"I was on that task force up in Denver."

"Right," Jeannette said on a sigh. "I should have taken your contacts there into consideration."

"Not seen me as the local, bumbling detective? Might have been smart because we *are* going to work together on this."

"Why?" Jeannette asked, her voice pleasant. "Why do you care so much about the drug ring?"

"I don't. At all. But I care an awful lot about the people you've snared in it. I think the boss-man in Dallas won't be too pleased to hear that your informant Donald and his wife are dead."

Jeannette remained silent.

"Which is why I'm telling you *right now* I have a warrant

for the Johnson residence," Sam continued, his voice somewhat pleasant. "I'm assuming you don't have the paperwork on file for me to work with another agency or entity; you go in there, I'll have to have you arrested."

"You are a world-class dick-wad," Jeannette growled.

"After the shit you've pulled this week and with *at least* Susan Johnson's blood on your hands, that would be you, Agent," Sam snapped back.

Hearing these two, Cici felt a cold spark up her arms. They were fighting about more than jurisdiction, but Cici didn't understand the real core of the argument. Unless…was this personal? Of course it was personal.

"I want information. Something to help me ensure no one else dies. You want the glory for the drug bust? I would have given that to you, anyway."

Jeannette scoffed. "Sure. Because you're so kind and generous. Everyone knows you're the department hot shot."

"I missed all the signs with you," Sam said, his voice soft. "But then, it never occurred to me that my girlfriend not only lied, but was *only* my girlfriend to further her career."

Evan flinched near as hard as Jeannette gasped. Cici took off down the hallway, unable to listen to more. Her heart ached for Sam—somehow, this entire situation kept getting more untenable.

Evan grasped her arm and tipped his head. They slunk down the hall to Evan's smaller but just as opulent office. He closed the door behind him and leaned against it.

"That was so awkward." Evan shuddered. "Way she was acting, that conversation would have gone south in a hurry."

"*Dios mio*, I don't even know how to process Jeannette…" Cici licked her dry lips. "Does everyone have a secret identity in this town? Who are you?"

"Just Evan Reynolds, Esquire. Tax attorney. I can't handle more than that. Especially not after that exchange."

"Why?" Cici asked.

Evan looked down at the plush carpet under their feet. He wore battered tennis shoes. Old ones. For some reason the slight peeling at the edge of the mesh endeared him more to Cici.

"I loved Anna Carmen. You need to know that." Evan blew out a breath. "But I liked her connections."

"Ah." Cici crossed her arms over her chest. "To our father. Thought you'd—what? Be governor one day?"

Evan shook his head, hard, once. "I wanted to be *the* tax attorney. Frank Gurule is known for helping those he chooses."

"Too bad you didn't understand how deep the rift ran between him and Anna Carmen, especially." Cici closed her eyes and leaned back against the door. "Aci and Mom were close—so close. Dad leaving…it destroyed their relationship."

"Figured that out," Evan said. He smiled and it was soft, lost in memories. "But by then, I was in love with your sister."

Cici flopped down into one of the visitor chairs. They needed a change of pace. Something to lighten the heaviness permeating their air.

"This investigation keeps growing," Cici said. "Like bad mushrooms."

Evan barked out a laugh. "Do I even want to know how the well-loved local reverend knows about 'shrooms?"

"Not from personal experience. At least, not the kind *you're* talking about. I meant the ones that pop up all over Sun Mountain."

Evan sat in his chair. "Sure you did."

"Um. So. I'm glad we have a minute," Cici said, leaning forward so her elbows rested on her thighs. "About Anna Carmen and your lost position in Scottsdale."

Evan waved a hand. "The job falling through was a blessing in disguise. I've heard things…"

"About that law firm?" Cici asked.

Evan nodded. "I don't mind working, but one hundred-plus hours every week for years to *not* make partner? No, thanks. I miss Anna Carmen, though." He blew out a breath. "More now that I know she didn't plan on dumping me—wasn't cheating."

"I'm here for you, Evan," Cici said. "Whatever you need to process the grief."

He studied her. "Sam's right," he murmured. "About you and your sister. Anna was the life of every party. Bubbly, happy, and easy to talk to. You're deeper."

Cici pressed her lips together. "Grief dug deep into my soul."

Evan's eyes lit up a little. Not enough to smile but this was a…an understanding.

"I don't doubt that. But it's more. It's…if there was one thing about Anna Carmen I didn't love, it was her desire to deflect what she didn't want to talk about."

Cici leaned back, but she nodded. Her sister became a master of deflection and redirection, which served her well with students but ended up making Cici feel lonelier at home. That was part of why she accepted the scholarship to Columbia for her undergraduate degree in the first place.

"You think Sam and Jeannette will be okay out there?" Cici asked, glancing back at the door.

"You want to go find out?" Evan asked.

Cici shook her head.

———

Sam tapped on Evan's office door a few minutes later, and from the tightness around his mouth and the angry sheen in his eyes, Cici decided now wasn't the time to ask how the rest of his conversation with Jeannette, the manipulative DEA agent, went.

Probably best not to bring it up at all.

Cici thanked Evan for his help getting them in the office. For the first time in over a year, she hugged him back, glad for the connection with another person who'd loved her sister as much as she did.

Still pondering the mind's ability to deflect grief and other unwelcome emotions, Cici followed Sam back out to his police-issued sedan. She sucked down the last of her ginger lemonade she'd ordered with her lunch, scrunching her nose at how watered down the beverage became in the heat of the car.

Sam drove with the efficiency and proficiency of long habit—a good thing, too, because his mind was clearly not on the streets or even his fellow drivers. Cici shut her eyes after the third close miss and prayed she'd arrive at their next destination in one piece.

"Did you know Jeannette worked for the DEA?"

Cici jumped and yelped. The car had been so quiet, almost

restful when she ignored the potential for an accident, and she'd been sliding into a light doze. Lack of sleep caught up with her, finally.

"No. I thought she was the mayor's executive assistant."

"She lied to me," Sam said.

His voice was soft, but Cici still heard the pain there.

"The whole time we were together."

"Maybe she had to. Maybe she felt she was protecting you or her job or the case or whatever."

Sam grunted. He flicked on his blinker and they turned onto the street with the low-slung adobe houses and stately trees. The large trees were what made this area so coveted. That and the oversize lots, the closeness to Canyon Road and downtown. A lot of checks for the real estate boxes, but Cici had always felt the houses here tended to be overpriced and sought out not for their seventeenth-century charm, but for the prestige of address—and elementary school. A source of unnecessary pride that stated most of the residents bought up the homes that the families who'd been there for generations could no longer maintain or pay the taxes to own.

Cici and Sam pulled up in front of Susan's double-adobe hacienda a few blocks from the Acequia Madre—a street named for the "mother ditch," a man-made tributary from the Santa Fe River used to irrigate the compounds and farms along this, the original stretch of Santa Fe.

"You know what I think?" Sam asked, breaking into Cici's budding melancholy.

She made an affirmative noise.

"I think Jeannette got off on lying. And you know something, Cee? I just…I'm beginning to think there's never a good thing that comes from lies."

"Look at what happened to the Johnsons," Cici averred. "Donald might have tried to make it right after the fact. But laundering all that drug money, if that's what he did, probably led to those deaths originally. I can't see how people think their omissions and falsehoods—whatever they call them, they're still lies—won't come back to bite 'em at some point."

"Does it make you angry?" Sam asked.

He stopped on the sidewalk, looking over at the Johnsons' large sand-colored home. Touches of an understated turquoise metal flashed in the large garden—wind sculptures purchased on posh Canyon Road, no doubt.

"What's that?" Cici asked.

"The fact that Donald's drug problem, his greed, cost Anna Carmen her life?" Sam replied.

"Yeah." Cici blew out a breath. "Yeah, that makes me really, really angry."

Sam tipped his head back to where Jeannette popped out of her perky little Prius.

"I have to go in here with her. See what we can see. She's livid, by the way. That her cover's blown wide open, which is going to make it harder for her to get another undercover assignment."

"I'm not sure what to say about that," Cici said, shoving her hands into the back pockets of her pants. "It's not like we went looking for her."

"That's the way of these revelations. You never expect them."

Sam's shoulders slumped as he shoved his hands into his pockets. Before he turned up the narrow brick path, he looked over Cici's shoulder. She turned, too, to see Miguel standing on his mother's porch, hands gripping the railing. He wore a bathrobe that hung open over a white T-shirt and flannel pants.

"Why don't you go talk to Miguel?" Sam asked. "I know you don't want to come back in Susan's house."

Cici shuddered. "I really don't."

"It's fine," Sam said. "Better you talk to him anyway."

Cici eyed Jeannette's rolling gait as she sauntered toward them. She caught Miguel's dark scowl.

"I definitely got the safer assignment."

Sam chucked her under the chin. "Keep it that way."

Cici picked her way between a couple of the cars parked on the roadside before ambling toward Miguel. As she moved closer, she noticed he wore work boots, still unlaced.

She glanced back toward the Johnsons' statement mansion once. Sam ducked under the yellow crime scene tape, clearly not willing to help Jeannette do the same.

Cici turned back toward Miguel. She placed her hands behind her back.

"You're looking better," Cici said. "How do you feel?"

Miguel nodded, his tanned skin lined with wrinkles around his mouth and eyes. Hard living for a man still in his forties. But then, grief created hard living.

"Like my body's trying to kill me. But then, I did almost die."

Like many native New Mexicans, Miguel's vowels were longer, his speech slow and steady. Cici's shoulders began to relax, enjoying the comfort and familiarity of the local idiosyncrasy.

"I'm glad you're okay, Miguel," Cici said.

"Thanks. And thank you for stopping by to make sure my mother and Juanito were doing good while I was in the hospital."

"I'm here to help. I hope you know that."

"Come on up," Miguel said, motioning her up the steps. "No reason for you to shout from down there."

"Are you sure about that? Last I talked to Juan, he seemed to think *I* was the problem."

Miguel made a dismissive noise in the back of his throat. She decided to take that as a positive sound, and she stepped up onto the porch. Miguel turned his dark gaze back to the Johnsons' house across the street, his scowl back, blacker and even angrier than before.

"I like you, Reverend. But that don't mean I trust you."

Cici held out her hands, palms up, but Miguel moved forward faster than she anticipated and flipped her hands over. His callused fingertip traced the red gashes on the backs of her hands.

"How'd you get these?"

"I had a run-in of my own. Probably with the same people who killed Marco."

Miguel closed his eyes. A thick, heavy breath slid from his nose. "How did you find out?" His voice was filled with exhaustion but also fear.

Cici tipped her head back toward Susan's house. "Susan. I heard Ernesto Espinoza murdered Rosalia." Cici bit her lip until the trembling in her chin ceased. "I'm so, so sorry for all you've been through," she whispered.

Miguel's dark gaze held hers, looking deep, then deeper still into her soul. Eventually, he nodded. "So you are. As I am for your loss. Rosalia…" He sighed. "I loved that woman, but she done messed up. Got my kid involved. That's not right."

"No," Cici whispered. "That wasn't right."

"Your sister? She tried to help Marco. At first I thought…" He dropped his head in shame. "I thought it was more than helping. Like…see, Marco adored Miss Gurule."

Cici's stomach twisted with a nasty feeling, but she, too, had read the stories of relationships between teachers and their students.

"That wasn't it," Miguel hastened to add. "Miss Gurule helped out all her kids."

That sounded more like the sister Cici grew up with, was close to. The slick ooze eased from her belly and Cici managed to breathe again.

"But Miss Gurule didn't know what she was up against. She and Marco were innocent of the ways of that sick world. People died who shouldn't have, Reverend. For no other reason than they learned too much about the bad seeds living here among us."

Miguel leaned against the porch, looking out at Susan's house with abject hatred.

"No way I'm helping that," he muttered.

"How about you help me?" Cici asked. "Please, Miguel."

The older man remained stubbornly silent, his gaze planted firmly between his unlaced boots.

"You heard the shots?" Cici asked.

"Yeah."

"And you called it in," Cici coaxed.

Miguel nodded, his hang-dog expression becoming even more hang-dog.

Cici raised her hand and set it on his tense shoulder. "You've had more than your share of hardship and yet, you've come out of it with such a kind soul," Cici said. "I'm in awe of you."

"You're a good woman, Reverend Gurule," Miguel said, but he didn't sound as though he believed anything positive would come from the call. Miguel scratched his head, causing his dark, gray-threaded hair to stand up about his face.

"Can you tell me what happened?" Cici asked, hesitant. "When Rosalia died."

Miguel turned back to stare at the house across the street. He was silent for a long moment. Then, he crossed the porch and settled into one of the chairs.

"You think it could save people's lives?" he asked.

Cici nodded.

"Not sure I care no more," Miguel said.

Cici leaned forward and laid her trembling hand over Miguel's.

"I'm really angry, too. They took too much. You lost your wife and child. I lost my twin."

She bit her cheek. Part of her expected Miguel to toss off her hand and stomp into the house. He stayed still and silent.

"I'm worried for Juan," she said. "For Jaycee. If people find out the kids came to see me." Cici's voice thickened with the worry and fear she'd tried so hard to keep at bay. "They shot my dog, Miguel. In the chest. He's…he might not make it. My dog.

On a trail. We aren't talking about someone who gives one damn about the sanctity of life."

As she caught her breath, her eyes went back to the house. Her body stiffened when Jeannette bee-lined from the house.

22

The love that follows us sometime is our trouble,
which still we thank as love. — Shakespeare

Cici's eyes followed Jeannette as Miguel ripped his hand free from hers. He scowled.

"You think I don't know that?"

Jeannette glanced over at them, her face unreadable. She opened her trunk and pulled out some items.

Cici craned her neck, trying to see what they were, but Jeannette was turned so that Cici couldn't see much more than her back. Cici made a grumpy noise because Jeannette knew Cici wanted to see.

"What's that gal got to do with this?" Miguel tilted his chin toward Jeannette. He still scowled, anger radiating off him in thick waves.

Cici shrugged. She didn't understand how, exactly, law enforcement worked, but the fact that Jeannette had been undercover meant Cici probably shouldn't share Jeannette's role in the case.

"Weren't they dating?"

Cici's face heated. She didn't like gossiping, but Miguel would remain fixated until Cici told him what he wanted to know, and she still hoped to find out about Rosalia, Marco, and her sister.

"I don't think that's working out so well," Cici said.

Many long moments passed. Cici began to despair that Miguel wouldn't say more about what happened to his wife and son.

"I don't have much else to tell you," Miguel said, staring off into space as if ruminating.

Miguel gestured for her to take a seat, so Cici settled into the flaking wrought iron chair next to Miguel's.

"I saw them, see," Miguel said. "At the prison. If I'd kept my mouth shut, maybe none of this would happen. But I didn't. Talked to Rosie and she got too interested. I didn't know then—not until well after my wife died that she'd been getting drugs from Ernesto. Tried to blackmail him into more drugs in exchange for some photo of the new girlfriend. Young gal."

Cici clutched her hands together on her lap. "As in underage?"

Miguel shook his head. "I don't know. I never saw the photo. But Marco did. So did your sister. Miss Gurule took it, Marco said. They're both dead."

Miguel crossed himself, lowered his eyes.

"And I was glad I didn't know. I needed to be here, to raise Juanito."

"I need you to tell me anything else you know," Cici urged.

"Why should I?" Juan's gaze tracked someone from across the street. "Your guy there seems like a good one, but I met my share of police, Reverend. I been on the right side of the law myself and what's it done me?"

Sam came up the steps with his hands in his pockets. "Want to add anything to the statement you gave earlier?"

"Nope."

"You heard from the penitentiary?" Sam asked.

Miguel glowered, as much of an answer as he was willing to give.

"I'll talk to the warden personally," Sam said. "Let him know what happened to you, Mr. Sanchez."

Miguel's eyes narrowed, his face turning thunderous before he swallowed and cleared his throat.

"Thanks, Detective. I need that job to pay Juanito's school fees."

Sam nodded, the frown continuing to mar the smooth skin on his forehead.

Miguel stood, a bit shaky, and turned to head into the house.

"Mr. Sanchez?" Sam called.

The older man stopped, his feet at the edge of the bright, multicolored doormat. He turned his head so that his hawk-like nose stood out prominently against the turquoise doorframe.

"Thank you. For calling in the crime. Especially after Susan and Donald treated your family so badly."

Miguel nodded. Cici caught a glimpse of a deep, unquench-able pain in his eyes. He opened the door to his home, muttering, "Goddamn gringos ruin everything."

Cici crossed her arms over her chest. "That was kind of you, Sam."

His eyes crinkled a little at the corners, but he didn't smile. He turned in time to watch Jeannette climb into her Prius. She shot Sam a hot, angry look that scorched Cici, who still stood behind him.

"I've been known to have a moment." Sam's voice seemed sadder than usual.

Cici tilted her head and squinted as if something began to percolate in her mind. Something about Sam she should know. Before she managed to catch the thought, his phone rang.

He looked down at the display and scowled as he answered, "Chastain."

He listened, and though Cici didn't hear the words, she could tell that the conversation did not appeal to Sam at all. He remained silent, his lips compressed before the scowl on his face blackened. He clenched his free fist and slammed it against his thigh.

"When?"

Again, Cici couldn't make out the words.

"Oh, he better."

Sam stabbed his forefinger at the "End" button and then clutched his phone in his hand, his eyes squeezed shut. He took a deep breath as he pressed his phone to his forehead hard enough Cici worried he'd leave a mark.

The creepy-crawly feeling slithered over Cici's skin. "What happened?"

"Justin's gone."

23

Things without all remedy should be without regard: what's done is done. — Shakespeare

"What?" Cici squeaked. "Wait. How?"

Sam tugged his hair free from its ponytail and ran his fingers through it, probably to stem a growing headache.

"I don't know."

Cici hustled after Sam as he strode toward his SUV. His gait remained stiff, his face showing just how frustrated he was.

She slid into the car and buckled her seat belt. After a long pause when Sam stared at the steering wheel, he slammed his fist against the dashboard once, then again. His lips formed an "ow" and he shook his hand.

"Things without all remedy should be without regard: what's done is done."

Sam started the ignition. With the slow careful movements that were so much more a part of him, Sam pulled out onto the street. "I don't remember that from the Bible."

"It's not biblical. It's Shakespeare. From *Macbeth*."

Sam grunted. "Not sure you choosing a line from a tragedy inspires me at the moment."

"Better than *being* the tragedy," Cici said.

Sam made another ugly sound in his throat. "We seem to be working toward that end diligently."

———

"Where to now?" Cici asked.

Sam turned right and pulled into the veterinary clinic. "We visit your dog, and I think."

"You're babysitting me."

He shot her a hot look. "You need it."

"Don't you have something police-y to do?" Cici asked. "I can visit Rodolfo alone."

Sam turned and looked at her, his shoulders folded in in dejection and his eyes opaque. "Truth? I got nothing, and I'm pretty fried over Jeannette."

Cici leaned in and hugged Sam. He dropped his forehead to her shoulder and kept his arms tight. Eventually, he drew back, his eyes still closed.

"Thanks."

"You bet."

Cici fidgeted. Finally, she got out of the car and walked up to the vet clinic's entrance. Sam beat her to the handle and held the door open for her.

"Aren't we a pair? I mean, I considered asking Justin to stay the night. Maybe then I would have been dating your prime suspect. Again." Cici had never been gladder about keeping silent than she was about *not* asking Justin to stay that night.

Sam put his hand on her arm before she walked in. "You wanted Justin to stay the night?"

Cici glared. "No." She swallowed but she didn't have any

saliva in her mouth, so she ended up coughing.

Sam shook his head. "That's right. You two dated back in… what was it?"

"Tenth grade. For about two months. Don't I feel dirty. Talk about falling for the bad boy."

"Years ago. I'm glad you didn't want him again now."

"I didn't," Cici responded. "Not after he dumped me for Aci."

Before Sam could reply, Cici greeted the young woman at the desk, who led them back to see the dog. This time, Rodolfo lifted his head and wagged his tail.

"Feeling better, boy?" Cici asked, crouching down to pet his ears. "Mona and I miss you."

"I don't think it's Justin."

"What?" Cici looked up at Sam. Rodolfo dropped his large head on her knee. Cici pet his ears, and he closed his eyes with a sigh.

"Whoever tried to hurt you the other night. *That* wasn't Justin. I'm not saying he played it smart—and yeah, I think it's his fault Anna Carmen's dead."

Sam settled onto one knee and pet Rodolfo's head. He spoke to the dog in a quiet voice. Rodolfo licked his palm, eyes closing at the bliss of Sam's touch.

"At least partially his fault. Justin's involved. Up to his eyeballs," Sam said, his voice meditative. "That's why he didn't rat his uncle out before. But he's not the killer."

Cici continued to stroke the dog's silky ears, enjoying the feel of his warm fur against her palm. "Let me have this one, Sam. I know I'm supposed to forgive. But for right now, let me have the anger. It's all that'll keep me going tonight."

Cici told Sam of her conversation with Miguel.

Sam nodded. "That's my next course of action," Sam muttered. "I need to find the girlfriend. I mean Ernesto's wife," Sam murmured. "Didn't we hear they married? Had a baby? Okay. That's what I need to focus on. Something tells me she's the constant here. More so than Justin."

"Why do you think that?" Cici asked.

"From what Miguel told you, the girlfriend knew Rosalia. Marco and Anna Carmen saw her picture. Donald either knew who she was or found out. I'm guessing he found out somehow and that's why he was killed once he knew."

"That's why Donald died fifteen months after my sister? Because of someone's identity?"

Sam pet Rodolfo's ears. "I'm not sure, but the woman's the central connection between all this."

"What about Susan?" Cici asked.

Sam frowned as he ran his fingers through Rodolfo's thick fur on his ribs. The dog's breathing wasn't as labored, and Cici hoped that meant he was improving.

"The killer worried Donald told her who the woman was."

"You think it's her? The girlfriend…wife…whatever." Cici waved her hand. Rodolfo whined, clearly unhappy with Cici's increased agitation. "You think she's the killer?"

His eyes flashed with concern. "Good question. I think she's the place we start. Because, Cee, as soon as word gets out that you spoke with Susan before her death, you're going to have a bullseye on your head."

Cici stopped petting Rodolfo's ears. Her entire body shuddered.

"You really think that?" Cici whispered.

Sam stood in a quick movement, his knees popping.

"Yes. I, do. Whoever she is…they're protecting her identity."

24

If I be waspish, best beware my sting.
— Shakespeare

Sam forced Cici to go back to the police headquarters for a third time—still not her favorite place. While Sam made calls, Cici offered to search the internet and social media feeds.

It's not like she'd be able to focus on her sermon anyway—the sermon she was supposed to preach tomorrow.

They had some leads—and a dedicated police escort for Miguel Sanchez and Juan until they found the killer—but they still didn't know the identity of Ernesto's crush-turned-wife.

"The warden is out of town. He said he's on a flight home and will get in touch in the morning," Sam said, rubbing the back of his neck. He hadn't put the elastic back in his hair, so now it slid forward, covering his face nearly to his jaw. He ran his fingers through it absently, much as Cici did when trying to alleviate an ache on her scalp.

"Why?" Cici asked.

"If we're lucky, the woman's name will be in the visitor rolls. If we're real lucky, the prison may have a photo of her from their CCTVs."

"What?"

"Closed circuit television," Sam said.

"Oh. Can't anyone tell us that? Like the secretary or something?"

"You want the secretary involved? Or talk to someone who is already involved—and maybe on Ernesto's pay roll?" Sam asked.

Cici shook her head. "No. I really don't."

Sam stood and motioned Cici in front of him. They walked out of the building and Sam collected his city-issued sedan.

"I want to advise you to continue to have a protector with you," Sam said. "Make it harder for the killer to get to you."

Cici agreed immediately, too scared and drained to put up any fight. Sam asked to crash at Cici's that night, unwilling to leave her alone and probably not that interested in being alone after his new revelations about Jeannette. Cici caught him a few times during the evening, looking down at his phone or frowning out the window.

They made it all the way through dinner and cleaning up the kitchen, both tense and jumpy. Mona picked up on their agitation and began to pace.

By the time Cici slid the last dish in the dishwasher, her head pounded from the tension there. Once again, she pulled out the freshly cleaned sheets and pillow and laid them on the couch while Sam used her bathroom. Once he was settled in for the night, Cici took a hot shower, letting the water soothe the worst of the kinks in her shoulders.

Wet hair dripping on her clean sleeping tee—she hadn't wanted to wake Sam with her hair dryer—she padded down the hall to her bedroom. She petted Mona before climbing into her bed. As soon as she closed her eyes, the dream leaped into her consciousness.

Cici was in Anna Carmen's body. The pain in her back took her breath and she couldn't scream as she sank to the ground.

Cici fought this moment—she didn't want to see it again—couldn't watch her beautiful sister die again. But the dream sharpened. Came into focus with crisper clarity.

And this time, Cici caught the flash of metal and pretty translucent beads from the glasses chain that swung out behind the person in the black coat and hat.

25

Cry havoc and let slip the dogs of war!
— Shakespeare

Cici woke with a start, her breathing as ragged as her thoughts.

Soft sunlight drifted in through her window, too bright, almost garish in its deep, bold blush across the eastern sky.

"No. Way."

Cici pressed her forehead to her raised knees.

No way.

Anna Carmen might not have known who the killer was, but Cici did.

What had Susan said? Something about perfume she couldn't place.

The flowers Carole brought to the hospital.

Bugged. Sam found the transmitter, the microphone buried deep in the stems.

But why?

She hadn't married Ernesto. Carole was a relatively recent widow. When had her husband died? While Cici was away—in her master's program at Yale, she thought. So, if not her...

Oh.

The woman Miguel mentioned was young, maybe still a teen

when they first met…Cici jumped from bed and slammed down the hall.

"Sam!" she called before she slid into the living room. His sheets and blankets were neatly folded at the foot of the sofa, the pillow placed on top. A note sat atop that.

Following a lead. Kevin Loomis will escort you to church. I'll find you as soon as I can.

Cici snatched it up, moaning as she did so.

Sunday. Church.

She had to deliver a freaking sermon when she knew who killed her sister—and possibly why.

Cici glanced at the clock and yelped, scurrying back down the hallway to get dressed.

She tried to call Sam as she pulled on her bra and blouse, but his phone went to voice mail.

"I had a dream last night. I'm pretty sure I know who killed—" Cici quit talking and instead cowered in the corner of her closet as footsteps sounded down her hallway. Mona hadn't barked.

Oh, no, not Mona, too. Please let her dog be alive, safe.

Then she heard a happy yip.

"Reverend?" a deep male voice said.

Cici practically melted to the floor in that moment.

"Be right out, Kevin," Cici called through her closet door.

"Okay. Sam said I needed to take you to the church. Doesn't your first service start in fifteen minutes?"

Cici wrestled into a pair of slacks and shoved her feet into a pair of pumps. No time to do more. She snagged her makeup bag and ran toward the kitchen.

"I need to let Mona out and feed her, and then we can go."

After letting the dog out, Cici rushed into her small office, grabbing the notes she needed with the liturgy lesson. One of her deacons was slated to read that—as had been set on the calendar for the past month.

Her musical and choral director worked over two months in advance, based on the liturgical calendar, so the music would be sharp.

Cici glanced down at her notes, her heart pounding. They were reading from the Gospel of Mark today. Cici bit her lip as she stared at some of the lines from the reading, "'Truly I tell you, people will be forgiven for their sins and whatever blasphemies they utter; but whoever blasphemes against the Holy Spirit can never have forgiveness, but is guilty of an eternal sin'—for they had said, 'He has an unclean spirit.'"

"You all right there, Reverend?" Kevin asked, eyes wide as she hustled back to the small kitchen.

No, she wasn't. Cici let Mona in and scooped out her food, letting it fall into the dog's dish without requesting the normal shake or down commands. Mona looked at her in askance before she shoved her head into her bowl and began to crunch away at the kibble.

"Forgot to turn on my alarm," Cici murmured.

"Oh. Okay. You just look like…"

"Let's take my car," Cici said. "You drive."

She tossed her keys to Kevin.

"I'm not supposed to drive others' vehicles in uniform, ma'am."

"Well, this is an emergency. I need to put on some makeup

so I don't scare away my congregants. If you get in trouble with Sam, I'll deal with it." Cici motioned an X over her heart. "Reverend's honor. Now, scoot."

Cici slammed the back door and locked it before hustling Kevin out the front. She made him drive while she attempted to put on lipstick and mascara. Not an easy feat with shaking hands in a moving car.

Kevin parked and Cici hurried into the church, running straight toward her office to grab her robe and stole.

Carole met her there. "I was worried. I thought we might have to cancel the service."

Cici froze, staring at the older woman for one heartbeat, two, before she shoved her arms into the white polyester robe.

"Overslept," Cici mumbled. "Bad dreams."

"Terrible business, all this going around. Have they caught Justin yet?" Carole made a deep sound in her throat.

"How are you related again?" Cici asked, studiously avoiding the older woman's eyes as she draped the stole over her shoulders.

"By marriage."

"Whose marriage?" Cici asked, striding past Carole. Her heart beat, thick and heavy in her chest. She was pushing her luck and she knew it, but she needed to hear Carole's side. Maybe…maybe this was just a misunderstanding.

"One of Justin's uncles married one of the girls in my family."

"Ah, that's right." Cici didn't turn around; she kept walking toward the sanctuary. She heard the piano music, saw Kevin standing awkwardly by the glass doors that led into the inner sanctum.

Cici dipped her head toward the young man, acutely aware of Carole behind her. Without another word, Cici, her knees shaking and her heart thrumming louder than any bass note on the piano, walked through the double doors and raised her hands as the crowd began to sing the first hymn.

She made it through the sermon—falling back on a previous one she mostly remembered from her time in Jamaica Beach. Thankfully, her congregants seemed to enjoy her abbreviated version, and were more than happy to stroll out of church early.

Cici glanced around but didn't see Carole.

"Kevin, will you walk with me to my office?"

The officer nodded. Cici cracked the door open, tensed and ready to run.

No one was there.

The note lay atop her Bible. The large gilt-edged version she typically kept on the credenza behind her desk. The book had been moved to sit in the middle of her desk and the paper was folded in half, upright so it was impossible to miss.

Big Tesuque. You have 20 minutes before I shoot Juan Sanchez.

This note was handwritten. Cici snatched up the note and ran to the vestibule.

No sign of Juan. Cici tried to regulate her breathing but she couldn't remember if he'd been at the service.

A bluff? Cici wasn't willing to take the chance—not with the Sanchez family who'd already been through so much.

A long dark ponytail striped with turquoise bobbed through the few remaining service goers.

"Jaycee!" Cici called, her voice cracking.

The girl turned, brows pulled low. One look at Cici and her eyes widened.

"Juan," Cici panted. "Was he in the service today?"

"N-no." Jaycee shook her head, voice trembling. "He went hiking with his dad."

"Where?" Cici asked.

"B-big Tesuque."

Cici bit her lip and shut her eyes.

"You're sure?" she managed to rasp out.

"Yeah. They were going to…I don't know. Bond, I guess."

Cici whirled around, slamming straight into Kevin Loomis. She shoved the note into his chest. He'd have the evidence needed to hopefully link this note to Carole via handwriting analysis. Finally, Sam would have something concrete to build off of. Cici shoved her other hand into Officer Loomis's pocket.

At his yelped, *hey!* Cici muttered an apology even as she wrangled her keys from his pocket. He stood there, gawping much like Jaycee was, as Cici turned on her heel and ran from the building.

"Reverend?" Kevin called just as Jaycee let out a low wail.

"Juan!" Jaycee cried.

She must have read the note Cici shoved at Officer Loomis. Cici didn't have time to comfort the girl. Instead, she shoved her way through her congregants, who stared at her, wide-eyed. She burst out the doors.

Cici ran to her car. Buckled in as she shoved the key in the ignition. Kevin ran toward her car as she backed out from her spot. Cici shook her head and whipped the car out of the parking lot, laying on the horn to get everyone to scatter out of her way.

Once on a main street, Cici wrangled her phone from her pocket and tried Sam again. The big jerk sent her to voice mail.

She punched the gas, shooting around slower cars, desperate to reach the hiking trail up in the Santa Fe National Forest in time.

"You better have a good reason to have your phone off, Samuel. I know who killed Aci," Cici yelled into the phone. She took a deep breath. "I'm going to Big Tesuque now. I…Carole's involved, Sam. I didn't *know*. I've told her about the investigation—just some basic things. I was feeding her information."

Cici's breath shattered.

"She said she's going to hurt Juan Sanchez."

Cici dropped the phone as she slammed on her breaks, breathing hard as she avoided rear-ending the car in front of her by an inch. She didn't bother to pick her phone up again as she wended her way up the side of Mount Baldy, hands clutched tight to the wheel as she said a constant prayer refrain.

Please don't let me be too late to save Juan.
Please don't let Carole hurt anyone else.
Please let Sam get my messages.

———

Cici exited her car as soon as she arrived. Nothing moved. She edged her way around the small building that housed the no-flush toilets. Cici stepped up the concrete steps to the flat, grassy expanse that served as the head to the trail.

The single lonely picnic table was empty, devoid of more notes. Nothing.

She walked with slow, careful strides through the thin rows of aspen and pine trees guarding the narrow path to the trickle of a stream.

Nothing.

Frustrated and unsure what to do next, Cici returned to her car with care.

She had no idea how close Carole might be to her car right now. She climbed back in and slammed the door shut. She locked it and gripped the steering wheel, trying to calm her racing heart.

She bent down and over the center console, trying to hold back a scream, when something struck her side view mirror, causing her to jump and scream. An arrow. With a piece of paper around the shaft.

With shaking hands, Cici managed to unroll the window and pull the paper from the arrow, leaving the metal tip embedded in the cracked glass.

You have ten minutes to get to the mile marker.

She couldn't take the chance of talking into the phone. Carole was a crack shot. Probably the person who'd shot Rodolfo. Cici never imagined her secretary, her friend, could hurt a dog. But, then, if Carole was involved, she'd murdered a seventeen-year-old boy.

Carole was definitely *not* the person Cici assumed her to be.

Cici's breath escalated as she rolled up the window. The mechanical whir hissed in seemingly slow motion.

Sam needed to know where she was. Sam would bring help. Cici couldn't wait—she could not let anything bad happen to Juan, to Miguel. They'd suffered too much pain already.

Cici glanced around as she pulled her hiking boots from her

bag. Good thing she'd worn slacks today since she didn't have time to change. That thought caused her to chuckle, which quickly turned into a near hysterical laugh. Why was she worried about flashing her butt to the trees and her would-be killer? There were more important things at hand.

Bending down to tug off her pumps, Cici dropped her phone onto the floorboards between the gas and brake pedals of her car. She sat up and settled her pumps on the passenger seat and picked up the boots she kept in a duffel bag in her back seat. She bent down and pressed the on-off button on the side of her phone five times in quick succession.

A gray screen popped up. Cici gulped as she slid the red SOS tab across the screen. With quick, efficient movements, she put on her socks and boots and managed to slide her phone into the right boot, under her sock.

She exited the car, aware of the light breeze ruffling her hair. Carole could shoot her, here, now. Cici walked forward.

Each step she took felt heavy, as if it were her last. She hurried up the trail as fast as she could move. Someone called her name. Cici froze as footsteps pounded up from behind.

"Thank god I caught you," Justin gulped, breath ragged and face flushed with exertion. His gaze darted around as he dragged her from the path into the stand of nearby aspens.

Cici began to struggle, twisting and trying to break free. She darted toward one side of a tree just as Justin captured her arm.

"Stop. I'm not going to hurt you. I swear, Cee. Listen to me. This is so much bigger than you think. Worse than you know."

Cici positioned herself on one side of a tree, most of Justin on the other side of the tree's trunk. His hands were wrapped around her wrist, but she thought she might have a chance to break his grip if she used the tree as leverage.

"Talk," she said.

"I tried to warn you. I don't want…Anna Carmen *never* should have died. That's why I went to talk to her."

"And Donald?" Cici snapped.

"He knew. He worked with Ernesto. Took a cut of the money."

Not new information, but Cici was putting the pieces together. J.R.'s warning came back to her. He must have become aware of the laundered money. That also explained why Evan lost his job offer and Donald was forced into retirement. J.R. needed him out of the firm to clean up his business and image.

"But why take Anna Carmen to see Donald?" Cici asked.

She glanced around, body stiff. Carole was here, somewhere nearby. Cici needed to keep moving.

"I thought Donald would talk sense into her. Explain what a bad guy Ernesto was—what he could do. But Anna Carmen told us she knew about Ernesto's wife. How she planned to use that knowledge as leverage. To ensure the safety of the rest of the Sanchez family."

Cici frowned, her mind feeling sluggish, unable to process the information. "I know, too."

"Ernesto, hell even Donald, protected her. His wife. And their son." Justin swallowed hard, his gaze darting around, too.

"I need to go," Cici said.

"It's not about the drugs, Cee," Justin gave her a shake hard enough to clack her teeth together. "Those are old news. The

DEA shutting down the operation isn't the problem. It's who takes the fall for it. *That's* what the killings are all about."

"The baby," Cici said. She gaped up at Justin. "If Ernesto's wife goes to jail now that Ernesto's dead, there'll be no one to raise the baby."

"Exactly. That's why you have to leave," Justin cried.

"I can't leave the Sanchezes here to be hurt because of me."

Cici pulled back, stumbling farther when Justin let her go. She fell over a tree root just as a multitude of gun shots rang out. Justin gasped and fell. Cici slid behind the tree, heart thrumming as her ears rang. Silence. At least, she thought it was quiet. Hard to tell with her ears ringing. She peeked out from behind the tree to see Justin clutching his arm to his chest, blood dripping between his fingers.

Cici scrambled forward, but Justin shook his head, hard. Eyes wild. "Run."

"I can't leave you," Cici gasped. "You're hurt."

More shots rained down, one clipping her bicep while more spat up the leaves and bits of rock and other debris into Cici's face. She turned her head and dove deeper into the woods.

26

One may smile, and smile, and be a villain.
— Shakespeare

Cici stopped running after she fell again, thanks to another protruding tree root. She lay on the ground for a long moment, trying to catch her breath. How long had she been out here now? Twenty, thirty minutes at least. Maybe more.

She stood on shaking legs and began to walk. She wasn't sure how long she walked overland or whether she was heading toward or away from the parking lot. She wasn't sure her car was safe, anyway.

On the plus side, she retained her phone—which was still at seventy percent charge—and her Camelback water pack.

The temperature began to drop, meaning another storm was rolling in over the mountain range.

She squeezed her arm with her free hand, trying to stop the slow drip of blood onto the trail. She staggered, trying not to fall into shock. She'd left Justin, wounded. Didn't matter if he was involved in Anna Carmen's death. Leaving him behind like that was wrong. Cowardly.

"About time you showed your face," a voice said in front of her.

Cici stopped, rolling up onto the balls of her feet. Her breaths came in short, sharp pants as her gaze slid through the thin white tree trunks, searching for the body to go with the voice. Though, she already knew who spoke, and her heart ached with the pain of that realization.

"Come on out, Cici. Much as I hate having to shoot you, better to get it done clean rather than leave you to bleed out like I did with Justin."

The shadow stepped into a narrow patch of sunlight and the revolver in her hand gleamed.

"Carole?"

"Not quite the bad guy you've been imagining, eh?" Carole raised the gun. "More of a Saul moment. No one ever expects the sweet little church volunteer."

The black hole that led to the chamber seemed to grow and Cici couldn't look away.

"What?" Cici choked. Was Carole insane?

"The drug show filmed in Albuquerque. *Better Call Saul.* You know."

Cici stared at her, heart fluttering against her ribs.

Carole shook her head. "Never mind."

"You shot Justin? Rodolfo?" Cici's breath caught on a sob.

"You weren't listening. The dead birds, the notes. You just *had* to keep searching for answers."

"You killed my sister," Cici gasped. "And I wasn't looking alone."

Carole's lips twisted into a vicious sneer. She lifted her gun.

"True, but I managed to bury the police investigation before, thanks to Justin. Your friend Sam wouldn't have managed to wrangle so much information out of people by himself. Not with all that glorious money and prestige people had to lose."

Carole's finger caressed the trigger. "Goodbye, Cici."

A body slammed into Carole, sending them both sprawling.

Justin rose, panting, on a growl.

"No more, Carole. You can't keep killing to protect Regina."

"Ernesto *did* marry your daughter!" Cici cried. The words burst out of her because she'd guessed that Regina must have been involved earlier—and Cici had tried to confirm her suspicions with Carole at the church. "Wait...how's Regina alive?" Cici asked.

Justin panted, his face coated in a sheen of sweat. His arm was wrapped in his T-shirt so his chest was now bare. The thin white cotton was already saturated with his blood from the wound in his arm, near his elbow. Cici couldn't believe he was upright, let alone trying to protect her.

"Not only is Regina alive," Justin panted. "*She* ordered her mother, Carole here, to kill Anna Carmen."

"No, she didn't. You know nothing. Shut up!" Carole screamed. She searched the ground for her gun, which must have fallen when Justin tackled her.

Cici remembered Gina in those last months before her death. Anna Carmen had sent Cici a picture of Gina's last week, where the young woman's skin appeared sallow with deep, bruised circles around her eyes. Cici had assumed the cancer treatment took its toll, but Cici had seen similar issues with the men and women who came to the shelter for food and a place to sleep. That group—the opioid addicts—never stayed long.

Many ended up in the morgue.

"Gina was hooked," Cici said. "On opioids."

Cici raised her eyes to Justin's. He fell to one knee, both his forearms resting there. His skin was sallow, his hair wet with sweat. He managed a brief nod.

Cici shivered, ringing her hands together.

Regina used drugs. Carole was the purveyor of illegal substances.

None of this made sense.

Carole, who'd been privy to Cici's schedule. Who knew probably more of the church gossip than Cici did. Who had access to the church computers and printers.

Justin took an unsteady step toward Carole. "You don't want the truth to come out? Too late for that, Tía."

Cici pressed her fingers to her trembling lips. "But…Gina killed Anna Carmen?"

"No!" Carole screamed. "*I* did. Just like *I* killed the boy. No one could know she was alive. *No one.* Not once she was involved with Ernesto."

"Rosalia knew," Justin puffed, his voice weak. He swayed, resting his hand on a tree trunk. The white bark smeared with red. "So did Donald, Anna Carmen, Marco, Susan, and now Cici and Sam and the whole SFPD. I called it in," Justin said.

Cici stepped forward, but Justin shook his head. "She married Ernesto before he went to jail. He was her only chance, see. He had the money for the experimental treatments."

Carole growled again, launching herself at Justin. At least she hadn't found the gun. Yet.

"I said stop it." Carole slammed her fist into Justin's chest. Justin grunted and swayed again, wrapping his good arm around the tree trunk to regain his balance.

"Ernesto kept her down in Cabo after he was arrested," Justin wheezed. "But Donald snuck her into the prison once, maybe more. I don't know. To tell Ernesto about…about the baby."

"You know nothing," Carole screamed.

"Miguel must have seen her. That's the only part of this whole situation I can't figure out," Justin said, his words starting to slur.

"Miguel suspected Ernesto was the man providing *his wife* with the opioids," Carole seethed. "He caught Regina with Ernesto when he went to confront him."

"And Miguel told Rosalia," Justin said with a nod. His eyelids drooped.

"Doesn't matter," Carole said. "It's in the past."

"My sister's dead, so many people died—a *child*, Carole! Because of your lies," Cici said. "I think it *very* much does matter."

Carole pulled a switchblade from her pocket. The handle was three inches long, black. The blade, when she flipped it up, was closer to five. The same blade Cici saw in her window the other night.

"You can join her in death and hug it out," Carole said, lunging at Cici.

Justin intercepted the blade, catching Carole's wrist in his hand. He dropped to his knees, clearly no longer able to stand.

"Get out of here, Cee," he gasped.

He tugged, hard, causing Carole to curse and hit him in his

bleeding arm. Justin fell forward, passed out.

Carole's eyes gleamed with triumph or hatred—Cici didn't know which—as she ripped her wrist from Justin's grasp. Cici bent and grabbed the closest fallen tree branch. Thankfully, it was only about three feet long with a few smaller branches sprouting from its length. She swung it and caught Carole in the arm before she could stab Justin. Carole slammed into another tree and faltered, sliding to her knees.

Cici ran to Justin, trying to help him rise.

Carole rose with a laugh, the gun she'd dropped earlier once again clasped in her hand.

Thrashing through the underbrush sounded from Cici's left, along with male voices.

"Reverend!"

Miguel burst from the trees. Carole raised the gun, but before she could shoot, Juan tackled her behind the knees from the other side.

Carole went down, screaming. She flailed turning over. She shot the gun.

Miguel grunted. He clutched at his leg as he slid to the ground.

"Papa!" Juan cried, lunging over Carole. She twisted and buried the knife in the boy's calf just as Cici rose, unsteady, and slammed the tree branch into Carole's back. Cici meant to aim for her head, but she was so shaken, she barely caught Carole's shoulder. The older woman grunted before turning and firing at Cici.

The shot went wide, the bark from the tree behind her exploding as the bullet hit the trunk. Carole advanced toward her as Cici tried to blink the bits of debris from her eyes.

Another bullet passed Cici's ear as she dove behind the dubious protection of the tree.

Carole simply walked around it as Cici scrambled away, trying to think of how she could save not just herself, but Justin, Juan, and Miguel.

Nothing came.

Cici's breath came in sharp pants. "How could you kill him? Marco."

Carole raised the gun higher, aiming for Cici's face. "It's not like I had a choice."

"There's *always* a choice," Cici managed to say.

"Not when your only child has stage three breast cancer at age nineteen, and you can't get insurance or cover the cost of treatment." Carole's chin trembled, and she blinked rapidly.

"You think I *wanted* to be related to a drug lord, Cici? I was a homemaker and happy with that lot. It's all I ever wanted to be. But my daughter needed help and no one—not the church, not my friends or family, *no one* would help her. Except Ernesto."

Carole's finger wrapped around the trigger. Cici took a deep breath and held it, wondering where she could go, if she had even a tiny percentage of a chance to survive Carole's attack.

Cici backed away.

"I'm trying to understand, Carole. Help me understand how you came to this point." Cici held out her hands in supplication.

"You don't care about my daughter. You're already over there, thinking I sold her body. But she'd be dead without Ernesto.

Now, she has money and prestige. She's a wealthy woman, free to marry who she wants."

"Did you…I bet you did." Cici gasped. "*You* caused Ernesto's boat to explode."

Carole's smile was brittle. "He wasn't right for my baby. He was simply a means to an end."

The woman before her was the worst devil Cici had ever faced—her single-mindedness caused her to destroy anything in her path, whether innocent child or do-good teacher like her sister.

Nothing mattered—nothing—except protecting her own child's life. A life built on others' blood and tears.

Cici's stomach heaved and she wanted to vomit into the stubby grass. Now wasn't the time for such luxuries. She needed a plan. She needed a firearm—not that she knew how to shoot. She needed a miracle.

Aci, if I ever needed you, now's the time.

A thick wind rustled through the leaves, causing them to shiver as a thick peal of thunder boomed close enough to make both women cringe.

Carole's finger squeezed the trigger and Cici dove to the ground.

The plus side was the bullet missed her. The down side was she struggled to scramble out of the way of ensuing shots. One bullet whizzed by her neck so hot the skin there sizzled. Another struck the dirt just in front of her hand as she yelped.

"In case you're wondering, I killed Donald and Susan, too."

Cici bit her lip but she had to know. "Did you call in Donald's murder?"

Carole's feet shuffled around the rock. The gun glinted in the afternoon sunlight. A large fly buzzed past the weapon.

"No." Carole smirked. "That was Jeannette."

"Jeannette. As in *Sam's* Jeannette?"

"No, you idiot!" Carole snapped. "*Of course* it was me."

Cici dashed away from the large rock, trying to get out of the way. Rain slanted into her eyes, making any moves more treacherous because the granite rocks slicked.

Carole didn't come after Cici because she now grappled with a large male.

"Stop it! You can't keep killing people." Justin's voice, thinner with the pain and blood loss, no doubt. But here was Cici's miracle.

Thank you, blessed Lord.

"You think you're going to play the white knight?" Carole snarled. "Anna Carmen's dead—dead in part because *you* didn't make sure she kept her pointy little nose out of my business in the first place."

Carole pulled the trigger again.

Nothing happened.

Carole screamed in frustration and charged directly toward Cici.

The wind surged and cold rain poured out of the clouds.

Cici scrambled backward. She stood on an outcropping, seeing that the ledge below her fell off another four, maybe five hundred feet. Nowhere left to go. Cici's heart ramped up to the same loud pounding as the raging in her ears.

I tried, Anna Carmen. I tried so hard to find your killer—to make sure you received justice.

She stared into the eyes of the woman whom she considered her friend. Probably the woman closest to a mother figure she had in years.

Anna Carmen's killer.

Carole launched herself at Cici. Cici darted to the left, but Carole grabbed Cici by the ankle yanking her with all her might. Just then, there was a sharper tug as Carole reached the end of the mountain. The ledge caught Carole in her mid-section, causing her to wheeze. Cici kicked as hard as she could.

But Carole's grip tightened as she slid to the edge. Down she fell, yanking on Cici's ankle. The bones there gave with a sharp crack as Cici scrambled with her hands, trying desperately to find any kind of a handle.

Nothing.

Her boot slid off, weighed down by water and Carole's grip. The pain caused Cici's mind to seize from pain.

Down they both fell.

Carole first, her scream of outrage and fear cut off.

Cici cringed, crying as she sought to grab the roots sticking out of the edge of the cliff face. She caught one, but the rough roots tore the skin on her palms and her momentum pulled her downward.

The air cooled as it seemed to speed up. Just then, Cici landed on one of the piñons growing out of the side of the mountain. It took her breath and scratched the skin on her back and ribs. But Cici managed to breathe in a deep sob. She looked up. Fifty, maybe sixty feet from the outcrop.

Anna Carmen glittered there, at the edge, her eyes wide and her mouth opened in a scream.

Her sister. Her savior.

———

"Cee!" Sam's plaintive voice reached through the roaring in her ears.

"Here!" She managed to call.

He looked over the side of the rocks, his face ghostly pale and his eyes wide. His short ponytail was undone, his hair flying around his face, sticking to his wet-slicked cheeks.

"You okay?" he asked.

"I—I think so."

Cici's voice remained much calmer than she'd anticipated. She dragged much-needed cool air into her lungs.

"Carole's below me. Somewhere."

"I have a full team. SAR and police. They've fanned out and are scouring the mountain right now. Let me focus on you."

"Good," Cici said. She breathed out deeply, trying to ignore the black tinges melting into her vision. "How'd you find me?"

Weren't the guys closer to the trail?

Sam's face paled, his mouth compressed. "I followed the screams."

Cici considered that. Probably he had, but she bet Anna Carmen helped as much as she could.

"I'm going to tie my rope," Sam said. He disappeared back behind the lip of the rocks. She heard other people calling up there, across the mountain. Hopefully, Juan, Miguel and Justin would get the treatment they needed.

Sam reappeared. His face taut with worry.

"Can you climb?" His voice held doubt.

"Yeah."

A rope dangled above her and Cici grabbed it.

"Wrap the end around your waist. Good, yes, just like that."

Cici's hands shook but she managed to knot the rope as she'd been taught by her search-and-rescue leader.

Sam's eyes stayed focused on her. She trembled with the relief of his nearness.

"Go slow. If it's too much, I'll pull you up."

"We need to find Justin, Miguel, and Juan," Cici said. "They're nearby."

She sucked in a deep breath as the damaged skin of her palms connected with the smooth nylon. Cici gritted her teeth against the difficulty of sitting up. Her ankle throbbed but she managed to pull herself up enough for Sam to grab her under the arms and haul her the rest of the way.

Then his arms were around her and his lips pressed to hers. He caught the back of her head and deepened the kiss as Cici began to collapse against him. He pulled back, his chest heaving near as much as hers was. He began to drag them both farther from the ledge.

Cici winced as her bad ankle—and shoeless foot—connected with sharp rocks and other debris.

Sam pressed her face against his chest. She curled her fingers into his wet shirt.

"You scared me, woman. And I'm so mad at you for not listening to me in the first place."

"Good Lord, Sam. You can't just kiss women you're mad at." Cici stumbled back and pressed her fingertips to her tingling lips. "And I did listen. I gave Kevin Loomis the note."

"You're hurt," he said.

"My ankle's a mess. Oh, and I got shot at."

Cici shivered in her sodden shirt, her one hiking boot squeaking as water sloshed around her toes.

Sam settled her on the rock and Cici tried not to convulse as she remembered what had happened here not long before. He wrapped her ankle with quick, efficient movements and checked her arm. The bleeding had stopped but the area remained red and angry. Cici winced when Sam prodded it with gentle fingers.

"I think this is okay," he murmured. "Anything else?"

He ran his hands up and down her arms, over her ribs to her hips. Cici winced when he slid his palm over the abraded skin on her back but she shook her head.

"Some scrapes. I'll be fine." She took a deep breath, wishing she could ask him about the kiss. But Sam continued to look her over, much as a doctor eyed a recalcitrant patient.

"I'm fine. Really. But guns are scary," Cici said, her teeth chattering. She clutched at her waist, trying to warm her frozen middle. "And loud. So damn loud."

"Always with the potty mouth," Sam said on a sigh. "And, yeah, having a gun pointed at you is scary."

He wrapped her in his arms and Cici rested her head on his chest again, breathing in the drying sweat and rain that caked his T-shirt to his body. He held her, rocking slightly, as one would a newborn. Cici soaked up his warmth and that of the sun peeking out from the dispersing clouds.

"Anna Carmen's been here this whole time, Sam. I know you don't believe that. And I understand why. But she helped save me. I'm sure of it. In my dream last night, she deciphered that note of hers. It's the mail boxes at certain post offices. Remember? 2 PS—that's Pacheco Street. We know about those. 3DVM—DeVargas—"

"Mall," Sam interrupted. He shook his head in amazement. "Oh, that's going to make this much easier."

"That's what you're going to take from what I just said?"

"I looked over the visitor books and saw the footage from the prison. Found out Ernesto was with Regina, Carole's daughter. That took longer than I wanted—and we almost lost you in the process—but you did good work, Rev."

After another long moment, Cici squeezed her eyes tight. "Can you help me down the hill? I want to get away from this place."

Sam threw Cici's good arm over his shoulder, bending at the waist to make it easier for her. Then, he began to shuffle down the path as Cici hobbled on one foot next to him.

"Just so you know, Cee, I trust you."

She heard the sincerity in his voice. His willingness to put faith in what he couldn't see brought tears to her eyes. She blinked them back with effort so she could focus on the trail. Cici had already fallen apart more than she liked. No reason to keep up the pitifulness.

They walked in silence; Cici hopped downward toward the narrow creek that sliced across the trail. "I need to check in with the team."

"I'm okay." Maybe if Cici said it often enough, she'd believe it.

Sam settled her on another large rock. This one had a flat top and no one trying to shoot at her. Cici sighed as she sank onto the surface gratefully. The faint rush of the stream hummed through the air, softer than the rippling waves of aspen leaves fluttering overhead. Cici turned her face up to the cloud-covered sun, her heart thudding with the thanks her lips had yet to say.

Sam stepped away and pulled the walkie-talkie from his belt. He spoke into the device.

"Thank you for what you did here, Anna Carmen," Cici whispered. "I—I'm almost sorry though. I would have gotten to be with you again."

Turning her head toward the stand of aspens back up the trail, Cici wasn't surprised to see Anna Carmen standing there. The white trunks of the trees were visible through Anna Carmen's body—she'd never be corporeal again. But she was here, looking out for Cici. And that had to be enough.

Anna Carmen smiled her brightest smile before she winked.

"Yeah, yeah. Always the trickster," Cici murmured. "I love you, big sis." The lump reformed in Cici's throat. "You have to come back and visit me again."

Anna Carmen's smile dimmed as she looked past Cici's shoulder. A snapped twig and a sharp intake of breath alerted Cici to Sam's approach.

Anna Carmen stepped forward, past Cici, much to her surprise. Before Cici could turn, Sam made a choked sound.

Cici faced him and Anna Carmen, but her twin no longer graced the small clearing. Sam looked shell-shocked, like he was fighting back tears of his own.

Cici closed her eyes and rested her forehead on her knees.

She was alive. Sam was safe.

"Any word on the guys?" Cici asked.

"They're all off the mountain," Sam replied. "And on their way to the hospital. None of the injuries are life-threatening, even Justin's, though he's lost a lot of blood."

Warmth warred with the sadness Cici experienced when Anna Carmen went to Sam and disappeared.

"Thanks for checking on them," she murmured.

Sam settled on the rock next to her and hauled Cici closer.

"I'm glad it's over. For them. And you, too."

They held each other as only survivors can understand.

Finally, they heard voices.

"Second wave of troops are here. We'll get you off this trail now."

"I'm not letting Carole take the joy of hiking from me," Cici murmured.

"We'll be back out here in no time," Sam promised. "You, me, and both your dogs."

Cici nodded. She stood slowly, against the onslaught of dizziness. With it came one small brush of a soft breeze, almost as if her sister were saying goodbye.

Cici's heart squeezed as she focused on the sensation. Sam met her gaze, his blue eyes clear.

A frown formed between Cici's brows.

"What did Anna Carmen communicate to you? I know she said something."

Sam ran his hand over his shorn hair at the base of his skull, a nervous habit leftover from their youth.

"She didn't speak, but I understood her." He met her eyes. "She said now's the time."

Cici's frown formed fully just as the first responders came into sight.

"Do you know what she meant by that?"

He shook his head slowly as though the effort pained him.

With that, he went to greet the rest of the officers who filled the clearing.

Cici closed her eyes and let the peace of the forest wash over her.

EPILOGUE

Lovers and madmen have such seething brains
Such shaping fantasies, that apprehend
More than cool reason ever comprehends.
— *Shakespeare*

Sam closed the file, a sigh of relief filling the near-empty police headquarters. He glanced at the clock. After eight. Most of the night shift was on patrol.

He opened his desk drawer and pulled out the ring he kept stashed at the very back, not in a typical black velvet jewelers' box but a cheap plastic pencil case. The edges were frayed with age and the plastic turning brittle enough to flake.

He pulled out the solitaire. Not a diamond because she never liked them. When he went shopping for a stone, he'd learned there were over four thousand minerals tucked into the earth's crust. Many he'd never heard of, let alone seen. The stone he chose was alexandrite, a purplish gem that flashed near emerald in the sun and closer to ruby in the dark.

Exotic, intriguing. Perfect for the woman who would never wear it.

"You were wrong, Anna Carmen," Sam murmured. "This is *never* going to happen."

He shoved the ring back into the bag, ignoring the small piece of paper, and zipped the pencil case shut. After shutting and locking his desk drawer, Sam stood and stretched.

He picked up Anna Carmen's file and slid it into his completed cases drawer.

After he shut it, he patted the cold metal once before turning and starting toward the door when he saw Evan leaning against the wall.

"What are you doing here?" Sam asked.

"Could ask you the same thing."

When Sam continued to frown, his heart racing, wondering how much of the last few moments Evan had seen, Evan stepped forward, hands up in supplication.

"I heard you talking. Mentioned Anna Carmen."

"Yeah." Sam swallowed the lump in his throat and forced himself to breathe normally. "She deserved justice."

Evan's eyes crinkled at the corners a bit.

"Congratulations on closing that case. I know it meant a lot to you."

Sam eyed Evan's relaxed pose. "You, too, I'd think."

Evan's lips curled up.

"Yeah, it did. That's why I came by. I needed to say thank you in person. Losing her...I talked to Cici for a long time last night."

Sam forced his feet to remain still. "Yeah? How'd that go?"

Evan tipped his head, eyes still watchful.

"Anna Carmen was a special woman. If I'd been smarter back in the day, I would have married her sooner. Told her I loved her more often. Assured her I trusted her judgment. Then, maybe, she would have come to *me* when she found out Regina was still alive."

"Blaming yourself won't change the past," Sam said.

"True. But I'm still trying to figure out how to let that go."

Evan paused, considering the younger man for another long moment.

"Anna Carmen talked about Cici a lot, you know. It's a twin thing, I guess."

"Yeah," Sam murmured, his heart hitching. "They were close, those two."

"Which is why I know Cici never planned to marry that guy—Lyndon? She was making noise about coming back to Santa Fe even before Anna Carmen died. Said she missed the people she was closest to."

Sam's chest ached. He replayed Anna Carmen's words in his mind: *You said it yourself, Sam. Nothing good comes from lies. Now's the time to tell Cici the truth.*

Sam chose not to answer. Instead, he grabbed his suit jacket from the back of the chair. After adjusting his shoulder harness, he put on the jacket.

"You going out tonight? To celebrate closing the case?" Evan asked.

"Yeah. With Jeannette of all people. I promised her a beer once she closed the drug operation. Seems like Regina probably won't get any jail time, not with Carole's confession up on the mountain that she'd killed Anna Carmen and the rest. And, from what we can tell, Regina wasn't aware of the lengths her mother went—or that Carole had killed Ernesto. She's fully cooperating with the DEA."

"Good," Evan said. He cleared his throat. "That's good."

Sam nodded, but his chest still felt hollow. "Fewer criminals roaming the street."

Evan dipped his head to his chest. "For the moment, anyway. I thought after your words with Jeannette…I guess I was wrong to assume you'd broken it off."

Sam paused in fixing his suit's collar. Not every day he wore a suit to the office. Not every day he closed a big case and met with the mayor, chief, governor, and the regional head of the DEA.

"Jeannette and I are definitely over. I can't trust her." Sam shrugged. "Plus, after closing this one—even with blowing her cover—I'm sure she'll get a plum assignment somewhere bigger than this town."

"Huh," Evan said, eyeing Sam with less pleasantness. "Well, I'm going to swing by Cici's place. She invited me to dinner."

Sam held Evan's gaze even though he knew he should turn and walk away.

"It's not like that. I just want to make sure she's handling the last couple of weeks all right," Evan said.

Sam shoved his hands into his pants pockets and refused to take that bait.

"You do what you need to do," Sam said. "I'm off to see Jeannette."

He headed down the hallway, but Evan's voice carried toward him.

"Tell her congratulations for me," Evan called. "And Cici, too. I'm sure Cee will be the first in line to forgive Jeannette her deception and hug her into the strange little family you two have developed."

Sam stopped. He turned to face the other man, his chest aching with the need to shout.

"What do you want, Evan?"

Evan stepped in close enough for his chest to brush Sam's. They were almost eye-to-eye, but Sam took great pleasure in the fact he was about half an inch taller.

"Same thing you did," Evan said, his voice quiet. "Maybe same thing you *still* do. I want the truth."

Evan's lips quirked up.

"All of it. And a happy ending for Cici wouldn't hurt, either."

ACKNOWLEDGMENTS

As always, thank you, Chris. Your unwavering support and love shine through in all you do for the kids and me. I couldn't ask for a better man, and I'm thrilled to wake up with you each day. You're also the best movie date a gal could ask for.

To Lisa Bateman and her husband Joseph Bateman, who put up with my slew of questions—and even my follow-up questions!—with humor and tons of knowledge. You made this book much stronger for sharing your expertise. Thank you.

To William Elias, who shared his expertise as a former police officer to make sure I had Sam's job description and time-frame on the force correct. Your expertise helped shape this manuscript—thank you so, so much.

To my family, thank you for your patience with my dream—and letting me hang out in my head *way* too often.

To my AuthorLab writing pals: You keep me on task and keep me motivated. I love your commitment and passion. I love reading your posts and stories. And I love how diverse our group is.

LERA ladies and gentlemen, thank you for being so supportive, for making me love writing again, and for sharing your knowledge so freely. You are the best.

To Heather Myers, thank you for seeing the big picture—and loving this book as much as I do.

To Nicole Pomeroy, thank you for being so detail oriented. I can't tell you how much I enjoy working with you because I know my books are so much better after your edits.

To my Divas, especially Lisa Bateman—you kicked ass with the eARC's and I can never thank you enough.

To Emma Rider, this cover is gorgeous. Thank you for sharing so much of your beautiful self in it.

And to my readers and reviewers. I would not be where I am today without you. I cannot thank you enough for sharing your time with me.

ABOUT THE AUTHOR

With a degree in international marketing and a varied career path that includes content management for a web firm, marketing direction for a high-profile sports agency, and a two-year stint with a renowned literary agency, Alexa Padgett has returned to her first love: writing fiction.

Alexa spent a good part of her youth traveling. From Budapest to Belize, Calgary to Coober Pedy, she soaked in the myriad smells, sounds, and feels of these gorgeous places, wishing she could live in them all—at least for a while. And she does in her books.

She lives in New Mexico with her husband, children, and Great Pyrenees pup, Ash. When not writing, schlepping, or volunteering, she can be found in her tiny kitchen, channeling her inner Barefoot Contessa.

CPSIA information can be obtained
at www.ICGtesting.com
Printed in the USA
FSHW02n2026140818
51448FS